"Vrabel presents a rare glimpse of what it is like to navigate new territory while legally blind. Alice's road isn't always an easy one, but her journey will be inspiring to readers, especially those who have struggled with a disability."
—*Publishers Weekly*

"Brimming with wit and heart, *A Blind Guide to Stinkville* examines the myriad ways we define difference between ourselves and others and asks us to reexamine how we see belonging."
—Tara Sullivan, award-winning author of *Golden Boy*

Praise for Beth Vrabel's *Camp Dork*

"Vrabel has a rare talent for expressing the tenderness, frustration, awkwardness, confusion, and fun of growing up. VERDICT In Vrabel's capable hands, the ups and downs of adolescence shine through with authenticity and humor."
—*School Library Journal*

"With good humor, Vrabel explores the pitfalls of emerging preteenhood. This quick read nonetheless effectively delves into interpersonal pitfalls that will be familiar to most older grade schoolers, and Lucy's developing insight may even provide a few hints for staying on the right path. Honest, funny, and entertaining."
—*Kirkus Reviews*

Praise for Beth Vrabel's *Pack of Dorks*

*"Lucy's perfectly feisty narration, emotionally resonant situations, and the importance of the topic all elevate this effort well above the pack."
—*Kirkus Reviews*, starred review

"Lucy's growth and smart, funny observations entertain and empower in Vrabel's debut, a story about the benefits of embracing one's true self and treating others with respect."
—*Publishers Weekly*

"Vrabel displays a canny understanding of middle-school vulnerability."
—*Booklist*

"A fresh look at what it means to embrace what makes you and the ones you love different. . . . *Pack of Dorks* is the pack I want to join."
—Amanda Flower, author of Agatha Award nominee *Andi Unexpected*

BRINGING ME BACK

Also by Beth Vrabel

Caleb and Kit
A Blind Guide to Normal
A Blind Guide to Stinkville
Camp Dork
Pack of Dorks

BRINGING ME BACK

BETH VRABEL

Sky Pony Press
New York

First Edition

This is a work of fiction. Names, characters, places, and incidents are from the author's imagination and used fictitiously.

Sky Pony Press books may be purchased in bulk at special discounts for sales promotion, corporate gifts, fund-raising, or educational purposes. Special editions can also be created to specifications. For details, contact the Special Sales Department, Sky Pony Press, 307 West 36th Street, 11th Floor, New York, NY 10018 or info@skyhorsepublishing.com.

Sky Pony® is a registered trademark of Skyhorse Publishing, Inc.®, a Delaware corporation.

www.skyponypress.com

10 9 8 7 6 5 4 3 2 1

Library of Congress Cataloging-in-Publication Data

Names: Vrabel, Beth, author.
Title: Bringing me back / Beth Vrabel.
Description: First edition. | New York: Skyhorse Publishing, [2018] |
    Summary: Ostracized after his mother's drunk driving conviction
    and his own behavior afterwards, twelve-year-old Noah begins
    making a fresh start while helping save a bear.
Identifiers: LCCN 2017047553 (print) | LCCN 2017057383 (ebook) | ISBN
    9781510725294 (eb) | ISBN 9781510725270 (hc: alk. paper) | ISBN
    9781510725294 (ebook)
Subjects: | CYAC: Middle schools—Fiction. | Schools—Fiction. | Conduct
    of life—Fiction. | Prisoners' families—Fiction. | Bears—Fiction. | Wildlife
    rescue—Fiction.
Classification: LCC PZ7.V9838 (ebook) | LCC PZ7.V9838 Bri 2018 (print) | DDC
    [Fic]—dc23
LC record available at https://lccn.loc.gov/2017047553

Cover design by Kate Gartner

Printed in the United States of America

For Jon
I love you

BRINGING ME BACK

CHAPTER ONE

November 5th

The bear rose on her back feet, slamming down to her front paws so hard the impact echoed through the woods. Head swinging, she pawed the dirt in front of me with long, sharp claws. A fierce, rumbling growl ripped through her and over me.

This was it.

We were both out of time.

About 2 months earlier: First day of seventh grade

I sat at the crumbling wooden bleachers lining the (former) football field, waiting for the first bell to ring. Picture this: me on the bottom bleacher by myself. My (former) best friend, Landon, and his (current) best friend, Mike, aka the armpit of seventh grade, on the top row just behind me.

They were talking about me and making sure I knew it.

And I knew exactly what they were talking about: the thing at the pharmacy over the summer. I still can't explain why I did it. I don't even like candy bars—they make my teeth hurt and my stomach burn. But I stole them.

My heart thumped in my ears, and it was like I was back there, shoving handfuls of candy bars into my pockets, watching my hands like they belonged to a different body, barely hearing the sound of the crinkling wrappers. I grabbed more and more, cramming them into the big pocket of my hoodie once my pants pockets were stuffed. I felt them break and bend as I cleaned out one box on the shelf and reached for a second.

It had been like I was in a trance, until the pharmacist noticed me and started yelling. I couldn't leave in time, and I couldn't explain.

The old man ended up not pressing charges, but of course the whole town found out. Like I said, it had been more than a month ago. But this was the first day of school, and everything seemed new all over again, including my almost-arrest. "Total loser," I heard Mike whisper-shout, "just like his mom." Landon didn't laugh, but he didn't stop Mike, either.

Whatever. I closed my eyes, pushing the heels of my hands into them, remembering how last fall, the night before the championship game, Mike jumped on a table and cheered when Mom and I got to Coach's party. Now Mom's in jail and Ashtown Middle School, a run-down, forgotten school in a run-down, forgotten West Virginia town, doesn't have a football team. And Mike, Landon, and the rest of the school won't ever let me forget that I'm the one to blame.

I don't know what made me look up, but when I did, I spotted her. A bear, hovering on the edge of the field.

Most people in Ashtown played it cool when they spot a bear—they weren't all that uncommon, especially around the edges of woods. But I couldn't pull it off. The part of me that wanted to yell *Check it out! A bear!* was at war with the part of me practicing being invisible. So I just watched her, pressing my mouth shut.

She stood her ground on the edge of the field, about fifty yards away. Once in a while, she looked over at me and the other kids hanging around the bleachers, but seemed to be doing her best to ignore us. She was small, but seemed fierce. We locked eyes for a second. *You don't have anything I want anyway. Stay put,* she seemed to be saying. I started to smile, but then Mike hopped off the bleachers, kicking up a cloud of dust. He picked up a rock and threw it at her. She backed up a step or two but didn't leave.

"What's your deal?" I snapped, fighting to stay seated. Mike outweighed me by at least ten pounds.

Plus, he's squeaky-clean to teacher eyes. If things turned sideways, I'd be the one in the principal's office. "She's not bothering you."

Mike huffed out of his nose and slowly reached down for another rock, this one roughly the size of a brick. "Got a problem, Sneaks?" he snarled. Like always, Mike cracked up as he said his stupid nickname for me, flashing super straight white teeth. He smirked as I pulled my feet back under the bleacher seat, hoping the dirt would finally cloud my vibrant red sneakers.

I glanced at Landon, but he just looked away, the side of his mouth pulling back. Maybe it was a smile, maybe a grimace.

"Don't worry," Mike singsonged. "I won't hurt the little teddy bear. Yet." He cupped the hand not holding the rock around his mouth and yelled across the field, "A month 'til bow season!"

The bear tilted her face toward him. Slowly, she took a small step forward. I had thought she was glossy black, but the sunlight revealed a grayish tint. A blue bear, I think they're called.

I recognized the heavy sigh behind us without needing to turn. Rina can expel her own hot air louder than anyone else in our class. More frequently, too. She spends summers in New York City with her father. She used to manage to drop that fact into every conversation, but for the past couple years, she didn't have to.

You knew she was thinking about it with every sigh and eye roll, and every day that she put on nothing but black, like she was in mourning. "That bear's practically a cub. You can't hunt a bear until it's at least seventy-five pounds. She's maybe sixty, tops."

Mike shrugged. "We'll see. Mistakes happen all the time."

"Do it and you lose your hunting license." Rina crossed her arms and glared at him. Her poofy brown hair swirled around her head in the breeze. It wasn't even September but it was starting feel like fall. "I'll turn you in."

"Tell on me and you'll lose more than that."

"What does that even mean?" Rina sighed again.

Mike twitched his shoulders and half-turned back to me. "Rina, is there jail time for killing the wrong bear?" He kept his eyes locked on mine.

"Of course not."

"Too bad. Noah's mommy and I could've been roomies."

I concentrated on breathing in and out of my nose so I wouldn't rush forward to punch him in his stupid all-American boy face, messing up his spiky blond hair and flattening his freckled nose.

Rina sighed again. "That doesn't make any sense, either. You'd go to a totally different jail than Noah's mom. Seriously, Mike. Maybe pick up a book once in a while? The black squiggles come together to form words, which form sentences, which form coherent thoughts. You could use a few of those." Rina stomped away from us.

Mike smirked. "Come on, Landon," he said. "Let's go."

Landon stared right at me.

And I stared right back. Neither of us blinked. Finally, the crunch of breaking twigs made us both glance toward the bear. A larger black shadow loomed in the woods just behind it—the mother bear, I guessed. "Stupid bears," Landon muttered as they disappeared into the woods. Like Mike, he mimed shooting his crossbow where the bear had been. He pulled on his backpack—the same battered one he'd had for the past few years—and walked off.

I tried to be invisible as time ran out and I had to enter the school. Crowds of kids belched out of arriving buses. For a second, I pictured Coach's whiteboard as he plotted out plays. I was the giant x sticking to the perimeter of the schoolyard, ready to flush into the end zone (my locker) at the last minute.

Even sixth graders whispered in scrawny huddles and glared my way.

My fists clenched, and for a second I thought about being like Mike, who lunged toward the newbies to make them feel as stupid as I felt. But the second I felt my nails dig into my palms, that echo of Micah Hardell's fall flooded my ears. Without wanting to, I scanned the crowds for the mass of space usually taken up by him, even though I had heard he switched schools.

Of course he wasn't there, big grin as he sputtered in his slow-moving way about whatever had him jazzed that week—space exploration, Star Trek reruns, super-hero comics. Of course I didn't see him. But I did see Rina, her eyes narrowed into slits as she stared back at me, like she could read my mind, maybe even feel the guilt oozing out of me. I remembered that she and Micah are cousins.

So I shouldered her glare, knowing I deserved it as I hid among the puny sixth graders, waiting to get into the school. But then, for some reason, she wasn't glaring. She smiled, like she would to a friend.

Finally the bell rang. I rushed along with the crowd through the open doors. My head down and shoulders curled in, I stepped it up as we passed the Office. "Mr. Brickle!" The throngs of kids separated around Miss Dickson, the plump, gray-haired witch of a secretary, as she bellowed my name.

I almost made it past her, too. But she has eyes like an eagle. "Noah Brickle!" she snapped. "Get over here! We listen when Miss Dickson calls us!"

I clenched my teeth and trudged toward her. Miss Dickson has this annoying habit of saying "we" instead of "you." Like we're all on the same side or something, even though she clearly hated anyone under forty. She glared at me with beady eyes under clumpy eyelashes.

"Mr. Anderson wants to see you." Miss Dickson licked her bubblegum-colored lips and tried to put her claw on my shoulder. I shrugged it off. Her nails dug into my skin for just a second. "Now, now, Mr. Brickle. We want to start of the year right, don't we?" She pointed to the chair outside the principal's office, and I slumped into it. Miss Dickson clearly got a kick out of kids being sent in to see Mr. Anderson. She's old school, thinking that going to his office meant, I don't know, a paddling or something. But really, Mr. Anderson is about as scary as Mike is smart.

The door was cracked, and I heard Rina's familiar heavy sigh trickle through. How did she get in there already?

"But this is the second year I've asked and the second year you've said you'd budget for a school newspaper next year. I only have one more year here!"

I coughed to cover a laugh a half second later when she snapped, "What do you mean *good*?"

"Rina, we have a strong English department already—"

Rina sighed. "Oh, really?" I heard her slam something onto Mr. Anderson's desk. "Each term begins with personal narratives. Every stinking year. Since *fourth grade*, I've turned in the same personal narrative about my ninth birthday. Every year. Look!" Rustling of papers. "It's the same essay. The same *A*. In two weeks, I'll turn in the same essay for the fourth time."

"Rina, you should be applying yourself more," Mr. Anderson half-yelled, half-groaned.

"You should be expecting more! I spent two weeks this summer at a journalism camp in the city." She said "the city" like New York was only one in the world. "I know what people my age are capable of doing, and we're not even close here."

Mr. Anderson's hand curled around the door as he pulled it open wider and stepped out. His voice dipped into his I-want-to-be-your-friend tone. "Listen, Rina, I appreciate your enthusiasm." For a second, his eyes drifted to mine. "I wish more of our students were as dedicated to making a *positive* difference. But unless you can drum up another student or two willing to spend their own time on the newspaper and a teacher open to overseeing the team, a student newspaper isn't in the works for Ashtown. We don't have the budget."

Rina stood in place. After a long pause, she crossed her arms. "So all I need is another writer and a teacher and I can do the newspaper?"

"That's not what—"

"Thank you, Mr. Anderson! I appreciate your support." Rina pushed pass me, leaving Mr. Anderson open mouthed.

I stood. "You wanted to see me, sir?"

Mr. Anderson stayed in the doorway and looked at me. "Come in, Mr. Brickle." He stepped aside, closing the door once I sat in front of his desk.

He sat behind the desk and stared at me with his hands folded under his chin. The bell rang.

"I'm late for homeroom," I said as my second glaring match of the day stretched another minute.

Mr. Anderson's lips totally disappeared as he pressed them tighter together. "How are you, Noah?"

I shrugged.

More staring. More silence.

Mr. Anderson lowered his hands, still staring at me. Mr. Anderson, you should know, has this strange ability to make kids just sort of spill out their troubles, scattering them across his desk for him to rearrange into something better. I used to do that. Last year, when Jeff made me go to school the day after Mom was convicted, Mr. Anderson had called me into his office. I spluttered like a baby, honking my nose and everything, while Mr. Anderson listened. But you know what? He wasn't able to do a thing with the messed up puzzle pieces I gave him. Couldn't turn anything into a better picture.

When I left his office, all I had were eyes as red as my stupid sneakers. So I wasn't going to fall for it this year.

"How are things with your stepdad?"

"Jeff isn't my stepdad." I sat on my hands.

"But you are living with him, right? Until your mom finishes her time?" The *until* seemed to bounce around the room. Mr. Anderson didn't seem to notice. "When is your mom's sentence up?"

Mr. Anderson loved football. He had trophies from when he was a high school quarterback all over his office. I wondered if maybe that's why he was a principal—like maybe the best moments ever happened when he was in his school so he picked a job that would keep him in school forever. No wonder he couldn't understand someone like me, who'd rather spend all day scraping the crusty black tar from the recycling bin than spend an hour in these halls.

I stared at one of his trophies, of a golden football, and shrugged.

"It's in a few months, right?"

I lowered my chin a fraction. "November fifth."

Mr. Anderson shifted. He leaned a little closer. This was his signature move, the one he always made right before smoothly pricking a kid's resistance to sharing all the details of his sorry life. *Here it comes.* Softly, Mr. Anderson asked, "Will you be staying in the district once your mother is out of jail?"

My head jerked toward him even though I didn't want to. Mr. Anderson continued, "Or will you be moving to a more . . . neutral area?"

I swallowed and shrugged again. No one had talked with me about moving. Jeff's engine repair shop is downtown. He wasn't going to move. No "For Sale" sign in the front yard. But everyone hated me here. They hated Mom even more. Jeff's shop was barely hanging on, even though the newspapers had pointed out again and again that he had left the party hours before Mom. How Mom and I moved in with him a month before she went to jail. The *Ashtown Press* even put him on the cover once, lauding him as a hometown hero for stepping up and taking me in so I wasn't shuffled into foster care, despite my "troubled behavior" following Mom's arrest.

A smaller article had printed beside that one on Jeff. It was all about the League announcing Coach Abrams wouldn't be coming back from leave. That he was too ashamed for serving so much alcohol at the playoffs party, which resulted in a player's mother being arrested for drunken driving. The League went on to drop Ashtown Bruins altogether, thanks to "lapses in judgment" prior to the championship game and "excessive violence" during the game. The "lapse in judgment"? That was Mom. The "excessive violence"? All me. And no one was going to forget it.

Since Ashtown School District is too poor to maintain a school football team without the League, that meant no one was playing ball this year. Because of me. Because of Mom.

My face flamed and eyes stung for a stupid second. Once Mom got home, Jeff would be free, too. Free of me. I never had thought about it that way before, but maybe the calendar he kept in the Shop, the one counting down days until Mom's release, wasn't for her freedom but his, when he could stop being a fill-in parent and go back to being himself.

"Jeff hasn't said anything about moving," I mumbled.

"What does your mom say about her future?" Mr. Anderson asked.

"I don't know."

"It might be helpful to ask."

I snorted.

"Well," Mr. Anderson continued, his voice heavier. "I think we need to assume you'll be sticking around then. I want you to feel like, no matter what, Ashtown Middle is a safe zone. A steady home." He leaned forward, hands flat on the desk. Again, my eyes left the trophy and faced my principal. Mr. Anderson's eyes locked me in place. "You need to know something, Noah."

Here is comes, the I'm-here-for-you-my-door-is-always-open speech, the one that ends with him putting out his fist for a bump and me having no choice but to do it. I sucked in my breath.

But Mr. Anderson's eyes were hard as stones. This was new. "I'm an understanding guy. Many of the students here view me more as a buddy than their principal. That's because I'll give you as many chances as you deserve, Noah. But you need to give a little back. Those stunts you pulled, they might not have all happened on school grounds, but that doesn't mean I'm not holding you responsible while you're here. Filling your pockets with candy bars at the pharmacy. Yes, I heard about your foray into shoplifting this summer. And what you did to Micah Hardell—a boy *you know* to be intellectually challenged . . . " Mr. Anderson shook his head, eyes never leaving mine.

"I told you last year that my door is always open to you, Noah. But I want you know that I'm going to be watching you. I have a responsibility to protect *all* Ashtown students."

Yanking my backpack off the floor and onto my shoulder, I stood. "Can I go to class now?" I whipped around, knocking three years of Rina's narrative essays to the office floor.

CHAPTER TWO

I pulled my schedule out of my back pocket. I'd missed homeroom. First period, life science with Mr. Davies. The door to his classroom was closed, but I could hear a deep voice seep out from under the door. ". . . the study of all components of life, from microscopic to observable . . ."

For a second, I just stood there listening to him. Jeff was way into science, always watching Discovery Channel specials. He'd gotten me into it, too, I guess, because I suddenly felt lighter than I had all morning. I eased open the door.

I thought through my play to get into class without anyone noticing: don't make a sound and don't look around for anything except an empty seat. Mr. Davies didn't pause his lecture, and I didn't stall by the door. I kept my head down and made my way to the back, where there was an empty desk in the corner. ". . . examining what motivates organisms to behave as they do . . ." I pulled the zipper on my backpack as slow as I could so it wouldn't be loud and reached for a notebook and pencil. ". . . For example, what pushes a student to think I'm not going to notice him sneaking into my classroom five minutes late for class?"

My heart thumped as twenty-four people turned in their seats toward me. I didn't look up, keeping my eyes on the faint blue line of my notebook. "I was called into the office."

"And your excuse is where?"

I swallowed. "Mr. Anderson didn't give me one."

"Here's another example, class, of what we'll be studying this year." Twenty-four bodies shifted toward the front again. I kept my eyes on the blue line. "Organisms capable of anticipating their own needs— such as a seventh grader able to realize he needs an excuse slip to interrupt a class—evolve and thrive. Those who lack that capability . . . well, they struggle."

I swallowed again, trying to ignore the crunch as my teeth mashed together.

"We'll give you a pass this time, Mr. . . . ."

"Brickle," I muttered.

"Brickle." Mr. Davies strolled toward my desk. He paused beside it. "Noah, right?"

I nodded, still not looking up.

"Where have I heard your name before?" I did glance up then, wanting to see if he really didn't know all about me already. Weren't teachers given files with everything bad about a kid before school started? You know, the permanent record Mr. Anderson was so fond of reminding us not to blemish. But as soon as I looked up, I wished I hadn't.

The corners of Mr. Davies's eyes crinkled as he scanned the other students and their whispered hissing about me. He was long and lean, thick blond hair slicked back and a skinny dark tie down his button-down shirt. Mr. Davies's hands were clean, nails neatly trimmed. I could see them well, as he leaned against the corner of my desk. His lips twitched. "Where have I heard that name before?" he murmured again. And I knew he knew. His brown eyes latched onto mine, daring me to snap or cry or react in any way.

A flash from the front of the room distracted me. Rina's hand shot in the air. Mr. Davies turned to see what caught my attention. "Do you need something, Rina?" Mr. Davies asked.

"I wanted to answer your question." Rina lowered her arm and folded her hands on her lap, waiting for Mr. Davies to give her the go-ahead, even as a few kids in the class groaned.

You deserve this, I reminded myself, closing my eyes to the image of Micah stained on my eyelids. I concentrated on breathing in and out, ducking my head and gripping my pencil so tight I felt it bend under my grasp.

"Go on, Rina," Mr. Davies said. "Why is Noah Brickle's name so familiar?"

"You probably read his name in the paper a year ago. When he won the math triathlon."

My jaw dropped almost as fast as my head jerked up. Rina's eyes floated toward mine for just a second, but her serious expression didn't change.

"No, I'm pretty sure that's not it." Mr. Davies rocked back on his heels. A couple guys laughed.

Rina nodded. "Okay. Then maybe you read his name in the paper all the times he made honor roll. I saw it there, next to mine." Rina's last name is Beltre, so we're always near each other in alphabetical listings. Last semester was the only time I hadn't made honor roll.

All around us, kids stared at Rina. Was she really standing up for me?

Leave it to Mike to ruin it. "Or, Mr. Davies, you read about his mother getting trashed and going to jail."

Chuckles broke out all around, the kids covering their mouths with their hands even worse than the ones, like Landon, who laughed outright. Rina's heavy sigh weighed down the room.

"I'm sure it was one of those things." Mr. Davies went back to the front of the room, and I went back to slouching over my desk.

Finally, I had just one class left. I gave myself a little pep talk. *No way it could be worse than lunch.*

Last year, lunch had been awesome. I had known no matter how late I got to the cafeteria, there'd be an empty seat next to Landon, who always packed and so got to our table first. This year, I dragged my feet. Someone must've gotten their locker mixed up with mine and dumped a bunch of papers and wrappers in it. By the time I had fished them all out and found the ticket with my lunch number on it, no one else was in the lunch line.

That was cool—the lunch lady gave me an extra serving of tater tots since it was the last lunch—but it meant all of the round tables in the cafeteria were already claimed. Trying to hold the tray, keep my head down, and zero in on empty seats sucked. I asked three different tables if I could sit with them. Each said no, they were waiting for someone. Even though I was the last person to the cafeteria.

Finally I found a table in the back, full of other would-rather-be-alone eaters, and each of us spent the last few minutes staring at our phones and pretending we were anywhere other than middle school.

At my locker again (and again clearing out scraps of paper—whoever thought they had my locker was a slob), I checked my schedule: advanced math with Miss Peters.

Great. Now I'd have to make another trip to the office to fix this mistake. I stepped it up so I could get to the class before the bell. I was lucky—no one else was in the room but Rina, already stationed front and center. At first I thought Miss Peters was another student, until I saw that she was wearing a staff badge and key around her neck. Her shiny brown hair was pulled back in a ponytail and, aside from red lips, I didn't think she was wearing any makeup. She smiled hugely when she saw me, which stopped me mid-stride.

"Um, Miss Peters? There's a mistake. I shouldn't be in advanced math." I handed her my crumpled up schedule, which she smoothed across her desk.

"No mistake, Noah." She smiled again. Seriously, if teaching doesn't work out, Miss Peters should sell toothpaste. "I reviewed your test scores and work from last year. You belong here."

I shook my head. I had failed every quiz the third quarter of school. I hadn't opened a book the whole month of April while Mom was in rehab, and barely managed to pass by June. My grades had tanked. I practically lived in Mr. Anderson's office. "But last year—"

Miss Peters's eyes narrowed. "It's a new year, Noah. Mr. Anderson and I both feel this is where you belong. Please take your seat." Though there were four empty rows of desks, Miss Peters gestured toward the one right beside Rina. I took the one behind her instead.

The room filled up. Brenna, this girl who had been on the cheerleading squad, was decked out in a too-short dress and about five extra layers to her face thanks to makeup. It was like now that the cheerleading squad had been disbanded, she morphed into a stereotype of what a cheerleader should be, like she was reminding us all of what she lost thanks to me. When she had been an Ashtown cheerleader, she actually had been kind of cool. Now, though, she hated me.

She stood in the doorway, rooted out some lipstick from her backpack, and smeared it on her lips. When she glanced up, she saw me watching and rolled her eyes. "Not a chance," she sneered. Mike laughed from his seat across the room. Another kid bumped her from behind, sending a line of cherry red up Brenna's cheek and scuttling her phone across the floor. "Jerk!" she snapped. She spent another minute staring into the makeup mirror, smearing at the lipstick streak with a tissue. When she finally looked up, the only seat left was right next to me.

"How are *you* in advanced math?" Rina hissed to Brenna.

"Mom made a few phone calls."

"I'm not sharing my notes." Rina turned toward the front and crossed her arms. A couple years ago, back when Brenna used to wear sports shorts and oversized T-shirts, Brenna and Rina were best friends. Then Rina called Brenna a sellout for sitting with the cheerleaders, which made Brenna start making fun of Rina, calling her snob. I wasn't sure who Rina was friends with now.

"I don't need your help," Brenna snapped. A little lower, she added, "That's what my tutor is for."

I kept my head down until class started, then did a quick sweep of the room. Looked like Landon didn't make the advanced math cut, making this the one and only class my former best friend and I didn't share.

How awesome this schedule would've been a year ago, the two of us sitting in the back of every classroom, passing paper rolled up like footballs, goofing off just enough to have fun but not get into trouble. Landon made the teachers laugh; I made sure our grades kept us off their radar. Landon had this way of charming even the bitterest teachers. Take Ms. Edwards, the English teacher, whose chair had to be molded to her massive frame, considering she never moved from behind her desk or looked up from her computer screen through eight months of classes. But last year, this *tee, tee, tee* of laughter tumbled out of the old toad when Landon recited a haiku about his toddler brother's potty training ("Splash! Fall into bowl/Aiming and standing is tough/When you're two years old.") I smiled into my fist, thinking about it.

"I'm telling you! I had it a minute ago!" Brenna suddenly squealed. She scattered lipsticks, pens, notebooks, and papers across her desk as she rooted through her bag. I had been so zoned out, I hadn't noticed the end of Miss Peters's waxing on about multiplying mixed numerals and the beginning of Brenna's freak-out.

"Someone must've taken it!" Brenna hissed.

I ducked my head again.

"Ask Noah," Mike shouted from the back row. "He's over there smiling right next her." A year ago, Mike had been on the outskirts of me and Landon, latching on to whatever we were joking about and bringing it up as we passed him the hall. Always trying to be in on whatever we were doing.

I slouched lower in my seat, feeling the prickle of everyone's gaze.

Miss Peters stood in front of my desk. "Noah, have you seen Brenna's cell phone? She's misplaced it."

"No," Brenna snapped. "I didn't *misplace* it. I had it in my backpack. Right here!" She pointed to the space between us.

I shook my head.

"Yeah, right," Mike muttered.

Miss Peters stayed put for another few seconds. I didn't look up, but I'm sure she was watching me, waiting for me to do something. Confess, I guess. I didn't move.

"I'm sure it'll turn up." Miss Peters finally turned around. "If Noah says he didn't take it, he didn't take it."

"But—" Brenna yelped.

"Enough." Miss Peters sat behind her desk. "I'm sure it will turn up."

Brenna groaned. "My parents are going to be so pissed." Somehow she made it sound like a threat. Rina sighed.

After the bell rang, I wasn't surprised when Miss Peters called me to her desk. I was sure she'd ask me to give her Brenna's phone, that whole innocent-until-proven-guilty thing an act for the rest of the class. But, just like Mr. Anderson, she surprised me. "Noah? Are you okay? Must be tough having everyone accuse you like that."

I bit my lip, but couldn't stop from saying, "Not like I don't deserve it."

"We all make mistakes, kiddo." She opened her laptop in a see-you-later sort of way. "Hope the rest of your day gets better."

I nodded, even though she wasn't looking. "Miss Peters?" I pointed to the classroom door, where just the edge of Brenna's cell phone peeked out.

"Noah!" Miss Peters clapped. "Why didn't you say something during class?"

I shrugged. Even if I had pointed out where the phone lay by the door, no one would believe me that it fell out of Brenna's bag when she had been pushed coming into class. They would've thought I had planted it or kicked it over there or something if I were the one to point it out. "I just saw it now."

"Oh, I'm glad!" And then I knew: she had thought I had taken the phone all along.

CHAPTER THREE

I walked to Jeff's shop after school. It was only a couple miles. I think Mom would've freaked out about it anyway, especially if she knew about the shortcut through the woods and the bear I had seen earlier at school, but I knew Jeff wouldn't ask how I get there. It's funny, I used to feel super lonely in the woods. When we first moved to Ashtown from Charleston, I was too used to living in apartments and always seeing other people around, and I wouldn't step into the forest for anything. Too quiet, too green. Landon used to bust me about it, the way I'd circle around so I could stick to sidewalks or the sides of roads. But now, the woods were the only place I didn't feel lonely.

Convey Auto Shop sits in the gap between two roads that lead into Ashtown's small downtown area. The Shop isn't much to look at—cinder block walls, cement floors, splatters of grease and motor oil—but the view is pretty sweet. Across the street is the river, with a long walking trail winding around it. It was close enough to Sal's, the pizza place, for us to have takeout almost every night (another thing Mom would've freaked about). And after Mom left, the guys in the Shop never stopped looking me in the eye or letting me ring up the cash register.

I found Jeff working under a shiny red Impala from the 1960s, the car's owner hovering nearby. "Hey, kid," Jeff said without pushing out from under the car. Guess he saw the sneakers. "How was school?"

"Fine," I mumbled. A long counter ran the back length of the room. Jeff had plugged a desk lamp in next to one of the stools so I could do my homework. I smiled when I saw the nameplate stuck to a space over the counter: NOAH, SCHOLAR AND ASPIRING CHESS CHAMPION. I guess I was aspiring, since I had yet to beat him.

"Nearing the top of the totem pole this year," Jeff said as I pulled up the stool and got out a notebook, acting like I had homework despite it being the first day. I had learned last year that if I looked busy, Jeff and the rest of the guys wouldn't ask many questions. "First day of seventh grade under your belt, buddy!"

"Whatever." I ran my pencil over the blank page, not paying attention to what I was drawing.

"Ah, come on!" Jeff pushed out from under the car. "I saw the way girls were checking you out last year." The Impala owner snickered like he knew me.

Yeah, I might be physically bigger than a lot of the

guys—in a tall, wiry way. And I guess I wasn't ugly or anything. Mom used to say my eyes and dimples were "a recipe for eye candy." But socially? There's the bottom of the totem pole, and then there's below the earth's crust. I hovered somewhere around the molten core.

"That was last year." The pencil point broke on the page. Jeff's engine oil-stained hands dug into my shoulders, turning me around.

Behind him was a giant calendar hanging from a nail on the shop wall. A giant black *x* covered each day that had passed. Each one reminded me that three pages in, a red circle surrounded a date—November 5. *FREE!* was written in all caps.

"It's been three months." Jeff was inches from my face, forcing me to look at him. I stared at the stubble around his chin, another thing that changed since Mom's been gone. She would've hounded him until he was fresh shaven. "Noah, three months since your mom . . . left. People will forget about it soon enough." His breath smelled like coffee and cigarettes. "Just stay out of trouble, man. Keep your nose clean. Kids have a short memory."

But Jeff was the one with the short memory. I had no trouble keeping track. I closed my eyes and took a deep breath.

Nine months and twenty-one days earlier, on December 1, Coach held the pregame party. That night,

Mom was arrested. Her face, a cartoon picture of shock with a circle mouth and backdrop of red and blue lights, flashed behind my eyelids. *Don't tell them, Noah!* Nine months and twenty-one days since Jeff burst through the doors of the state police barracks, arguing with an officer that he could take me home, that they didn't have to call Child Protective Services.

And that meant it'd been nine months and twenty days since the championship game. I could still hear the crunch of Micah falling, still could see him flying away from me, still feel the impact as I tackled him full force. I could still see his face, crumpled behind his helmet. I could go right back to the moment when I realized he wasn't getting back up. When I realized I had wrecked everything.

Then the dates get a little mashed in my mind. But I know about a week passed before a police cruiser pulled up in front of the apartment Mom and I had lived in then. And then, a couple days later, I waited outside in the lobby of a public defender's office, trying not to hear Mom's sobs.

And then January 5, when I sat in the last pew of the district magistrate for something called a "prelim," which I'm still not sure about but I think is like a test run of a trial. Mom sat up front next to the same tired-looking lawyer, before the judge. Next to them was a woman in a black business suit. Slowly, I had realized she was the prosecutor and I was the child she was talking about when she talked about endangerment and neglect. When she talked about severing parental rights, she was talking about Mom's rights *to me*. Other words didn't have as much effect on me, but they definitely did to Jeff, who choke-coughed when the prosecutor said the words "third offense" and "felony."

I remember Mom standing, her shoulders shaking, when the judge said Mom had four months to get "her affairs in order," to "figure out guardianship for her minor child," to attend parenting classes, and enroll in "a suitable twenty-eight day detox."

And that meant it was eight months and sixteen days since we broke our lease and moved out of the apartment with its dripping faucet and patch of grass in the middle of town and into Jeff's bungalow on the edge of it. A week of Mom saying there's no way they'd really make her go to jail, that this was all a big mistake we'd figure out. That finding space for everything we owned in Jeff's little house was something we'd have done eventually, anyway. That this timing was "just in case." And so was that meeting with the social worker and Jeff being the one officially in charge of me for school forms and permission slips.

While we're doing math here, that means it's been four months and twenty-one days since April 1 (April Fools' Day, not that anyone but me noticed), when Mom left for rehab. "Think of it as test run," she had whispered as she hugged me goodbye, "for next month." And that's when I knew she had been lying to me along. That this wasn't a mistake.

And now we're finally at the three months, like Jeff said. But technically, it'd been three months and seventeen days since May 5, the day the circuit court reconvened. That day my mom once again stood in front of a judge across from the prosecutor. The day my mom pled guilty to a reduced charge of second offense of driving under the influence of alcohol. "Do you understand that this comes with a mandatory six-month sentence in regional jail?" the judge had asked. My mom had nodded. And I realized I hadn't told her anything she needed to know—that I loved her. That she needed to stay safe. I hadn't told her that. And as an officer put Mom's narrow wrists in handcuffs and led her from the room, as Jeff shook in the pew next to me, I realized I didn't have anything to say her after all. Nothing at all.

Three months and seventeen days since I've seen my mother.

It sounds like a long time. It felt like a long time. But it wasn't.

The Impala guy cleared his throat, but Jeff didn't move, just kept staring me in the eye.

Jeff sighed when I didn't blink. After a too-long

moment, when the rest of the shop seemed blanketed with our silent stare off, he went back to the car. I grabbed a different pencil and again just sort of ran it across the page, not really thinking about anything in particular. Without even realizing it, I had sketched the blue bear from that morning.

Glen, Jeff's chief mechanic, roared a laugh from just behind me. "Goin' on a bear hunt?" Glen rasped. He snagged the notebook from the counter and held it under the fluorescent light like it was the *Mona Lisa*. Jeff won't let anyone light up in the Shop, but Glen still had a cigarette between his lips, bobbing up and down as he spoke, just waiting for the next break.

I shrugged. "I saw the bear hanging by the school this morning."

"They're becoming a nuisance round here." Glen rolled the cigarette between his lips. "Used to be you'd only see 'em deep in the woods. Now they're all over."

"Can't blame them," the Impala owner piped in. "We're taking over all their land. Makes me sick. Plus, idiots leave trash out all the time for them to forage."

"Huh." I looked over at the man. He didn't strike me as someone who'd fight for animal rights. He wore a suit that looked about a size and a half too big and was drinking the free coffee from one of the Styrofoam cups Jeff leaves out for customers. The guy looked more like a salesman than a tree hugger.

"What?" Impala guy stared at me so hard a line formed between his eyebrows.

I shrugged. "You just don't seem like an animal lover. Actually, you don't look like the type to care all that much about anything but that car." As soon as the words left my mouth, I wished I could've crammed them back in. The man's frown dug deeper than that line between his eyebrows. All I heard in the shop were Glen's wheezy breaths for a few seconds.

"*Noah.*" Jeff sighed.

Finally, the man's frown broke and his lips curled up at the sides. "The kid sweet-talk all your customers, Jeff?" He laughed.

Jeff stood and wiped his hands on a rag. He walked over to ruffle my hair. "Only his mom's sponsor."

"Wh-what?" I stammered.

The Impala man put his hand out to shake. "I'm Mr. Trenton. You can call me Trenton, though."

I stared at him. "Why does Mom need a sponsor? A sponsor for what?"

"For help and support managing substance abuse issues." Trenton smiled like he was talking about frolicking puppies or something. I turned away and Trenton moved with me, so he was wedged against the counter in front of me. "Addicts like your mom, they need someone to look out for them, someone who's been there."

"So you're an addict, too?" I sneered.

Trenton grinned. "Yep. Like your mom. I've been sober for more than ten years, though. I'm part of a group called Honor Healing For Recovery. We work with people to help them stay sober and out of trouble. My goal is to ease your mom's transition back into society and her family when she's released in a couple months. I'll check on the two of you from time to time. Thought I'd come out and see the lay of the land. She sure misses you, kid."

"Why would you need to meet me? I'm not the addict."

Trenton snorted.

"What?"

"All struggles are family struggles," Trenton said. "It's not like this is a cakewalk for you, kid." Trenton sidestepped so he could see Jeff. "Thought I'd get an oil change from my old buddy, too. Used to play ball together in high school."

"Shouldn't you have a badge or something?" I asked.

Trenton grinned, his blue eyes crinkling in the corners. Suddenly he almost seemed like a nice guy. "I'm not a prison guard or anything. Just a regular guy, so just regular clothes for me." To Jeff, he added, "He's just as blunt as Diane."

Jeff smiled down at the cement floor. I wondered if his stomach got punched every time he heard Mom's name, the way mine did. "They're cut from the same branch."

Those words, *cut from the same branch*, echoed in my ears. But when Mom and I were side by side, no one could tell we were even related. People used to ask if she was my babysitter. For the first time ever, that felt like a good thing. If we moved, like Mr. Anderson suggested, no one would even know she was my mom . . .

"Whatever," I mumbled.

"Anyway, Noah, your mom said you'd gotten into some trouble—had sticky fingers at the pharmacy this summer," Trenton said. "Pinched a bunch of candy bars, right? Well, I'll tell you, that fits right into the profile for children of incarcerated parents. In fact, a number of studies say parental incarceration is the biggest threat to a child's well-being in the United—"

"Trenton!" Jeff jerked his head toward me. He cleared his voice. "Noah was never charged with anything there."

"Oh. Right. Sorry." Trenton shrugged. "I need to choose my words better. Always running at the mouth."

"No filter," Jeff said, sounding like Mom.

"So, Noah, there's a teen meeting over at the Baptist church on Tuesday nights. We have this van that comes round. Could pick you up and you could talk—"

"No." I grabbed my notebook back from Glen and sat down hard enough to make the stool rattle.

"It's a good group," Trenton said. "About fifteen kids." When I didn't say anything, Trenton cleared his throat. "I can see that talking too much isn't a problem with you."

I didn't respond.

After a moment, Glen slowly sank into the seat next to me. He ran a hand through his short gray hair. "How big was he?"

"Who?" I grunted, not wanting to talk.

"Your bear."

"Still practically a cub," I said, thinking about what Rina said. "Too little for hunters this year. But it's a blue bear."

Glen laughed, a hoarse, sandpapery chuckle. "Some folks used to say I looked more blue than black." He held out his big hand, turning his dark skin in the light.

I laughed, but the sound rattled around the shop. Trenton studied his coffee. Jeff kept rubbing at his hands.

I'm not sure why people get weird whenever someone talks about skin color. It's not like Glen went and decided to be black or Trenton opted for white and Jeff decided to be something in between. People just are what they are.

"If you see that bear again, be careful, kid." Trenton dumped his coffee cup in the trash can. He nodded toward my sketch.

"Ah, come on." Glen chuckled. "Black bears are about as dangerous as a puppy dog."

Trenton puffed air from his nose. "Tell that to the college kid who got attacked hiking in New Jersey last year. Black bears attack a person every year in North America."

"You're like a walking Wikipedia, aren't you?" Jeff tossed the rag he was using to clean his hands onto the counter.

Trenton knocked the side of his head with his knuckles. "Steel trap." Turning back to my drawing, he said, "And if it's a blue bear, better believe hunters will be aiming for that pelt."

Hunting was a big deal in Ashtown. Like, school closed on the first day of deer season. Trenton was probably right about the bear.

"Yeah, but this one is little," I said, even though I didn't want to talk to him.

Trenton leaned down, resting his elbows on the countertop next to me. "Then you really need to worry. 'Cause its mama is probably lurking in the shadows."

Jeff went back to work under the Impala as he and Trenton started talking about Mom's upcoming release. About what she could and couldn't do after she got out.

"Even after she's done the time, there are lasting consequences. After all, this was officially her second

DUI conviction, though we both know it was actually her third. And she had been driving with a minor in the car. So her license is gone for five years. Another violation during that period, and she's doing more hard time," Trenton said. "Have you thought about putting an IID in her car?"

"A what?" Glen broke in.

"A 'blow and go,'" Jeff's voice, soft and steady as old jeans, floated up from under the car. "Ignition interlock device. Car won't turn on if it detects alcohol on Diane's breath. And, no, Trent. I haven't. I trust her."

Trenton shrugged. "The stats—"

"She learned her lesson," Jeff cut in.

"That doesn't mean she won't have lapses."

Jeff's whole body stilled under the car. "She'll never drive drunk again. Never put Noah at risk again."

Trenton and I made the same *hmmf* noise at the same time. He grinned at me. I didn't smile back.

Jeff pushed out and pointed to Trenton. His face flared. "*I'll* make sure Noah's never at risk again. I left him there—"

"I told you, man," Trenton said, "you've gotta let go of the guilt. She made the choice, not you. You can't keep making decisions out of guilt."

"Enough," Jeff snapped as my head flooded with thoughts too fast to sort. "Move on."

"All right," Trenton said with a sigh. Then he ranted

on about more meetings and "recovery paths." I tuned them out.

You can't keep making decisions out of guilt. Decisions like taking me in? Was Jeff only keeping me out of foster care because he felt bad for leaving me behind at the party with Mom that night? I bit my lip, trying not to think about it and not being able to think of anything else.

But then Jeff was standing right behind me, and I heard him say, "I'll let Diane know when Noah and I see her on Saturday."

Glen's face flashed toward mine and then to the ground, but he didn't say anything.

"You tell her. I'm not going," I said. Jeff and Trenton ignored me. Louder this time, I said, "I'm not going there." Trenton's eyes narrowed, but he didn't say anything.

Jeff turned toward me. He sighed, his shoulders rising and falling and breath tickling the back my hair. I concentrated on my drawing, shading in the bear's back. "Come on, Noah. Cut her some slack."

"I'm not going," I repeated.

Jeff's arm moved out, his hand hovering over my shoulder like it was deciding whether to land. Times like this, I know what he's thinking: *If he were my kid, I'd* . . . Fill in the blank. Slowly, he lowered his hand back to his side.

Trenton mumbled something about getting more coffee. Glen muttered that he'd brew a fresh pot. Jeff stood there, just behind me. I pressed so hard on the bear outline that the paper tore through. I scribbled harder when Jeff spoke next, trying to scratch out the sound of his words. But I couldn't.

"Do you know what it's like, Noah, every Saturday when I go there? Her eyes, searching for you. Smiling, a little, for me, but searching for you. Can you picture her? Noah, come on, man. She's your mom. She made a mistake—"

I shot up so fast the stool fell backward, clattering to the ground as Jeff hopped out of its way. I rammed past him, hitting him with my shoulder. But I didn't have anywhere to go, so I just took a new seat in the waiting room. The seats are comfier there, anyway.

I squeezed shut my eyes, but couldn't mush out Jeff's words, stop them from rattling around my head.

Next to me, this tiny twerp squirmed in his chair, humming a *Sesame Street* song about counting to three and pushing buttons on his mom's cell phone. The mom sat with her arms crossed, glaring alternately at the garage bay where her minivan was getting tuned up and the clock, which seemed to be moving extra slow for both of us. A baby in a carrier snoozed at her feet.

"*A, b, c, d . . .* " The little kid started singing the alphabet. "*h, i, j, k, Elmo doesn't pee . . . q, r, s . . .* "

I glanced at the mom, but she didn't smile or correct the kid. She didn't even hear him, too busy glaring into the garage.

I put my head on my knees, trying to think of the bear, of Rina, of Landon, of anything but my mom. In that moment, I couldn't even think of what I'd had for lunch that day, or what I'd gotten for Christmas last year, but somehow I could remember every bit of a throwaway hour with my mom when I was the squirmy preschooler in a waiting room chair. I could almost smell the lavender from her shampoo as she wrapped her arm around me to whisper in my ear. (Do they let you have special shampoo in jail?)

This was before we knew Jeff, but it was a repair shop a lot like this one. Walls covered in posters of motorcycles. Huge windows overlooking the workrooms. Coffee pot spitting in the corner. Mom beside me, not scowling toward the next room or distracting me with a phone. Leaning into me so we were one person on two chairs, whispering a story to me about talking cars that only listened to a certain little boy, waving off the mechanic and his clipboard when he said our car was ready. "Let me finish telling my boy a story," she said, not looking away from me. *My boy*, that's what she always called me.

CHAPTER FOUR

That Friday, Mr. Anderson called every Ashtown Middle School class to the auditorium. The space is alternately known as "the cafeteria" and "the gymnasium," kind of a one-room-fits-all. Ashtown isn't exactly a well-to-do town. Our county is top in the state for two things: the worst water quality and highest unemployment. So the school makes do a lot, including the all-purpose auditorium. Basketball hoops hung from two ends of the room, and we sat on the floor since the cafeteria tables were still stacked in the back. That morning, homeroom teachers had said that the assembly would be held outdoors, but then it started drizzling. It was pretty obvious the cafeteria workers weren't happy about the change in plans. Ladies in hairnets hurried by with trays of chicken nuggets, and custodians stood by the stacked tables, waiting to spring into action.

"All right, students," Mr. Anderson began from a little stage at the front of the room. "We have a few announcements as we kick off what is sure to be the best Ashtown Middle School year yet!" His voice boomed at the end and he pumped his fist in the air like he expected a chorus of hoots and cheers. Instead, a couple teachers clapped once or twice around the perimeter of the room.

Mr. Anderson then went over the same rules we've always had since the beginning of kindergarten. No hitting. No kicking. No back-talking. No cheating. Near the end of this annual speech, all of us started shifting, gathering up books and eyeing the door. Then Mr. Anderson took a deep breath, letting it out into the microphone so it puffed across the room, blanketing the fidgeting. "One more thing," he said. "This year, I feel I need to emphasize something more. I want us all to be *good citizens*." He said this part slower and quieter, which somehow made the words louder in my ears. "What does it mean to be a *good citizen*?"

Of course he didn't really want an answer, but Rina's hand shot into the air anyway. Mr. Anderson ignored her. "It means doing what's *right*. What's *honest* and *good*. Citizenship means seeing wrongdoing and doing your part to end it. It means to never, ever benefit from taking what's not yours." I couldn't drop my head fast enough to miss Brenna's face whipping toward me. "It means helping students when they need it and never, *ever* being cruel to those who are different." Again I felt the heat of a hundred eyes on me. An image of Micah,

crying, flashed behind my closed eyelids. I rubbed the
heels of my hands into my eyes to scatter the picture,
but I couldn't block the crunch echoing in my ears.
Mr. Anderson's voice droned on. "We look out for our
own and uplift rather than tear down. This year, more
than ever before, I will personally be seeking out good
citizens. And I will be doling out severe consequences
when I see students being *poor* citizens. We're just
beginning a brand-new school year. It's a fresh start.
Let's all act accordingly."

Mr. Anderson's gaze swept across the room, snagging on me for a beat too long. I shook my head a little.
I think he seriously thought he was helping me out and
reminding everyone to be nice to me, when really he
was just highlighting all the reasons I was an outcast.

As everyone started shifting around again, Mr.
Anderson held up a narrow hand. "To finish our
assembly, some students would like to make a few
announcements."

At that, four girls headed to the stage, Brenna leading the way. They wore Ashtown Bruins cheerleading
uniforms, and each carried a bucket. They giggled in
that annoying girls-who-know-everyone-is-watching
way. I nearly sighed, but Rina, seated two rows ahead of
me, saved me the trouble. A little buffer of space separated Rina, just like the bubble around me.

"So," said Brenna, popping out her hip so her little

cheerleading skirt flared. "You all know that, this year, we don't have an Ashtown Bruins football team, even though last year we *technically* won the championship, right?"

Actually, *technically* the game was forfeited, thanks to me. I realized the crunching sound in my ears was my teeth grinding.

"Thanks to some *poor citizenship,* as Mr. Anderson would say"—she flashed a grin at the principal, who suddenly looked a little uncomfortable—"our team's standing is gone, along with our coach." Brenna and the other two girls popped out their bottom lips in stretched-out sad faces, and I threw up in my mouth a little. "But we're not going to let that keep us down, right?"

Behind her, the other two girls spirit-fingered and cheered, "Right!"

They clapped and pranced around the stage, moving way too much for just piling the buckets into a little pyramid. "Here's what we're going to do, Bruins!" Brenna punctuated each word with a peppy little clap. "We're going to fill our buckets!"

To their credit, most of the audience groaned, remembering the push in elementary school to "fill each other's bucket with kindness." Was this going to be some cheer-laden bucket o' kindness drive?

"Here's the deal," snapped Brenna, dropping the

façade for a second and speaking in her usual don't-mess-with-me-or-I'll-tell-my-mom tone. "At the end of this season, the League is having a meeting to plan next year's teams. We're going to apply to be reinstated!"

Mike and Landon hooted, and a bunch of other kids cheered.

"Now, for it to work, we've got to show we're serious and ready to make big changes to avoid how things went last year! So we're having a fund-raiser. We're going to raise five hundred dollars!" Brenna shook her pom-pom for no apparent reason and jumped up and down a few times. "It will show the League that we get what happened was a big deal." Pom-pom shake emphasis on *big deal.* "We're going to donate all of the money to a charity of the League's choice, in the League's name. They chose MADD—Mothers Against Drunk Driving."

All the air left my lungs with her sucker-punch words. I stared hard at the gym floor but couldn't block out Brenna's voice. "If you're nominated by someone in the morning announcements, you've got twenty-four hours to dump a bucket of Gatorade over your head and donate $10 to the fund! It's going to be so fun!"

"Gatorade?" Landon called out from the back of the room. Few kids in Ashtown, Landon especially, could afford full-priced Gatorades, let alone convince their folks to buy them just so they could dump them over their heads.

"Or any energy drink," one of the cheerleaders chirped.

I glanced up at Brenna. She put her hands on her hips and stared at Landon. "It's like when the football team won a game and the team would dump a cooler of Gatorade on the coach and sometimes even the MVP of the game." I'd been MVP plenty of times, and I shuddered a little, remembering the shock of liquid and ice rushing in a wave over my head. Mom would grumble and laugh all at once about spreading a towel across the back seat before I could get in the car to go home—or, more likely, out for pizza to celebrate.

A few people around me shifted further away, like they knew what I was thinking.

"Well," continued Brenna, hoisting up a huge poster from the stage floor with help from the other cheerleaders, "if you help us 'Bring Back the Bruins,' you're *our* MVP!"

"Bring Back the Bruins" was plastered across the sign, with a bucket of orange stuff being dumped onto a cartoony bear mascot. To the side was a bigger, blank bucket with lines along the side, marked 100, 200, 300, and 400, with 500 written across the brim of the bucket. "Whenever we get a donation, we'll fill in the bucket a little more! Mr. Anderson is letting us hang this in the hall."

"Isn't that kind of stealing?" Rina loudly asked. "I mean, from the ALS fund-raiser a few years ago."

Brenna scowled at Rina, who smiled pleasantly back. "ALS used ice water. We're using Gatorade."

"Or any energy drink," the other cheerleader piped in.

"Come on, everyone!" Brenna shook her pom-poms again. "We have until the League meeting—November fifth—to fill our bucket!"

November 5. The date circled in red and labeled *FREE!* on the calendar at the Shop.

"That's less than three months, but we can do it!" Brenna and the other two girls clapped in sync and moved into a little triangle formation. In a chant, they said, "Give me a 'B'! Give me an 'R'! Give me a 'U'!" The girls lost steam at the lame, splattered response. Someone in the back, an eighth grader who wouldn't be able to play on the team anyway next year, shouted, "Give me a 'Shut up!'"

But then Landon hopped to his feet. "Come on, guys!" he shouted. "Let's do this thing!" He threw his arms out like he was fanning a fire upward.

Brenna grinned, and the girls repeated the cheer. This time, just about everyone hopped to their feet and shouted the team letters, ending with a booming, "Let's go, Bruins!"

"First challenge: Mr. Anderson!"

I had to get out of there. As I snuck out of the room, one of the girls filled one of the buckets with generic energy drinks, while another spread a plastic tarp under a foldable chair. Brenna pulled a smiling, in-on-it-all-along Mr. Anderson from the crowd. He grinned and shook his head in protest, but trudged toward the chair, pulling two twenty-dollar bills out of his pocket.

I was halfway down the hall when I heard the splash and responding cheer.

Mr. Davies's face flushed red. "Survival of the species depends on trial and error," he spouted mid-lecture. He really got into this stuff. Even though it was the end of the day, he was as fired up as Jeff fresh from downing three cups of coffee. Mondays kick off with science. Fridays, the day ends with it. My schedule was created by the devil.

"The error leads to the gradual elimination of characteristics. The trial leads to leaps and bounds. Literally! Think, for example, of the first fish to develop legs!"

I couldn't believe no one was calling him on out this bull. Like a fish one day just decided, "Okay, let's sprout some legs!" And *boom*! Legs. I squeezed my teeth together so hard my jaw hurt to keep from raising my hand. I guess maybe Mr. Davies was right about something. Earlier he had said the urge for self-preservation supersedes all other instincts in an organism.

Mr. Davies kept right on going. "Now that guy had some bragging rights. Where would any of us be without him?"

"Or her," Rina muttered.

"Right, right." Mr. Davies smiled indulgently. "Yes, a female fish followed, of course, solidifying the evolutionary shift."

If looks could kill, Mr. Davies would've been pulverized. "*Or,*" Rina said, "the female fish was first and the male fish followed. You know, if things happened as you say, with one fish one day popping out some legs instead of thousands upon thousands of tiny evolutionary shifts that eventually, over the course of generations upon generations, led to growth of leg pods."

I choked on a laugh but heard a chuckle anyway. It was Landon, perched in the farthest seat from mine. Out of habit, maybe, his eyes locked with mine. Out of habit, again, I grinned back. Landon's smile dissolved into a scowl.

"Yes." Mr. Davies grimaced. "I was trying to explain the situation in a casual, fun way, Rina. But—"

A ping over the loudspeaker cut into Mr. Davies's sure-to-be-witty reply. "Mr. Davies, sorry for the interruption. We need to see Noah Brickle in the office immediately."

"But school lets out in five minutes," I said.

"Better bring your backpack." Mr. Davies smirked.

Miss Dickson's bubblegum-pink lipstick was smeared in the corners, probably from twisting her lips together, trying not to look happy when kids get in trouble. "We have a seat when we are called to the Office, Noah," she said.

I went to my usual spot—the empty seat outside of Mr. Anderson's office.

"No, not that one. This one!" Miss Dickson pointed instead to the seat in the front lobby.

"What's this about?" I asked.

Miss Dickson picked up the phone instead of answering, pointing to the chair and twisting her lips some more. She punched a few buttons on the phone and soon was ordering shipments of paper clips and copy paper.

I kept my eye on the clock. School let out in three minutes. Then I'd be free.

Miss Dickson added manila folders to the list. "The kind with varied tabs, not all tabs at the same spot. Yes, that's important. Very important." I was pretty sure the quality of Ashtown Middle School education depended on proper varied-tab manila folders.

One minute.

"Add three four-packs of dry board erasers. What? Since when? Okay, so I'll take four three-packs . . . "

Forty seconds.

"Yes, that's it for now. Friday? Fine. We'll make do with what we have until Friday." Miss Dickson shook her head, like she was making a huge sacrifice, waiting a week for the erasers, folders, paper clips, and paper. She went to hang up the receiver, then jolted it back to her ear. "What do you mean you need the account number? It should be on file!" Her eyes, thick with mascara, flitted toward me.

"No . . ." Her voice dipped. "No, I can't give you the account number right now. I'll need to call you back when I'm more . . . secure." Now she openly glared at me.

I felt my face flame.

Thankfully the bell blared. Miss Dickson hung up as I rose to my feet. "See you Monday, Miss Dickson."

"Get back here, Mr. Brickle. We are not dismissed!" She twisted her glossy lips.

"I'm going to miss my bus!" I stopped in the doorway, halfway in the office, halfway toward the exit. I could taste the freedom in the bus exhaust floating into the lobby.

"Don't you lie to me, boy. I know you don't take a bus. I've got eyes everywhere." Miss Dickson got up so her palms pressed against her desk. "Get back to that seat."

I slumped back. "What is this about?"

More lip twisting. "About this." Miss Dickson slapped a pile of paperwork onto the desk. My name was written across the top, the rest of the forms blank.

I sort of recognized the back-to-school forms, since I had a crumpled-up copy of each stuffed in the bottom of my backpack. "You failed to return a single form. They're due back today."

"I'll bring them back Monday. Sorry, Miss Dickson." I grabbed them from the desk, but she tugged the papers back out of my hands.

"Too little, too late." She jabbed an electric-blue fingernail back to the chairs. "I've already called your father. I mean, your guardian. You can't leave until these forms are signed."

"You what?" I groaned and threw my bag down on the chair. "Why would you do that?" The Shop is buzzing right after school, and I knew Jeff had a packed schedule. I helped book an appointment for a three-thirty oil change. No way would he cancel last minute just to fill out some stupid forms for me. Jeff wasn't going to be here for at least a half hour. And when he got here, he was going to be mad.

Miss Dickson twisted her lips some more and pointed to the empty chairs. I slunk into one, arms crossed.

Ten minutes later, the door flew open and Mr. Anderson strode in, followed by Landon. "Another missed bus." Mr. Anderson jabbed his thumb toward Landon, then jerked his chin toward me. "What are you doing here, Noah? Everything okay?"

Before I could say anything, Miss Dickson snapped,

"I've got it under control, Mr. Anderson. I think you're probably still needed at dismissal." Right on cue, the clattering of books hitting the ground and someone cursing rang out. Mr. Anderson backed out of the office.

"Have a seat." Miss Dickson pointed toward the only other empty seat in the lobby—the one right next to me.

"Aw, come on!" Landon slammed down his bag and turned so his body faced away from me.

Miss Dickson punched another couple of digits into her phone. "Yup, he missed the bus. Again." She paused, glaring at Landon all the while. *Again?* I guess Landon always had been sort of forgetful. Like he never did his homework unless I bugged him about finishing before we went out to play ball. But he never missed the bus last year. I chewed my lip. Maybe he never missed because I had always been there, in the seat next to him. Miss Dickson sighed, breaking apart my thoughts. "All right. I'll let him know."

After slamming down the receiver, Miss Dickson crossed her arms and twisted her lips some more. "Might as well get comfy, Landon. Your mom says she can't come and get you until your brother wakes up from his nap. And heads up—she's not happy." Miss Dickson sure seemed so, though, judging by her gleeful smirk.

"Aw, come on!" Landon's hands curled into fists.

After a couple minutes, resigned to our fates, we both got out our homework. It was strange. Like I knew he hated me. He did everything he could to make that clear when we were in a group of people, laughing when Mike shouted, "Sneaks!" before the assembly this morning, shouldering me into lockers in the hall, coughing out curse words in the cafeteria when he passed me. But when it was just us, he wasn't spewing hatred anymore. He was just kind of sad. He flicked his pencil against his work sheet. I glanced at it—math. I bit my lip to keep from telling him he was solving the problem in the wrong order.

Landon used to come over to Jeff's house after school. Even though Mom and I had our own place, we had dinner at Jeff's every night, so I'd just go there after school. Plus it was only two blocks away from Landon's house. We'd down chocolate milk while we plowed through our math work and his little brother, Henry, played with trucks on the floor under our feet.

Landon babysat his little brother all the time, which meant that when he came over to do our homework, Henry came along, too. Mom ate it up, loving on Henry with tons of kisses. One time, she sang this song about Henry being her honeybun, sugarplum, and all these other horrible words moms use to torture chubby-cheeked babies. Henry covered his ears with fistfuls of trucks, whining, "I wish I had earlids so I couldn't hear you right now. That'd be the time of my life."

I didn't mean to, but I snort-laughed out loud thinking about it.

"You got a problem?" Landon snapped.

I glanced over at his math homework again. He still was way off. "No, but it looks like you do. You've got to get the denominator down to a whole digit before you can multiply the fractions."

Landon glared at me.

"Like this," I said, shoving my paper toward him. I thought he'd just copy the answer, but he didn't. Landon wasn't like that, even the Landon that hated me.

"Why is that two-fifths? Isn't it this plus two?"

I squinted down at his work. Landon had covered the margins of his paper with numbers that didn't have anything to do with the problem. That was the thing with him, I remembered. Word problems screwed with his mind. Any extra information swiped his focus. He always forgot to just focus on the problem. "You've got to simplify," I told him, ripping a fresh sheet of paper from my notebook and writing the equation across the top. "Ignore the stuff that doesn't matter. First you've got to—"

Again, the door flew open. "Noah!" Jeff rushed forward, eyes wide. "Are you okay? I got a message to come in right away, but I was under a car and—"

"I'm fine, Dad. I just…" The word *Dad*, it flew light
as air out of my mouth but landed like a brick between
us. *Dad?* Why had I said that? Jeff's mouth twitched
and head tilted away from me a fraction. "I mean, I just
forgot to fill out some forms."

Miss Dickson cleared her throat. "The papers are
right over here."

Jeff turned toward her, mouth still a little agape.
"Paperwork? I got a message that I needed to come to
the school immediately *for paperwork*?"

"All students are *required* to have papers filled out
by their guardians. *All* students." Miss Dickson crossed
her arms as Jeff took quick strides toward the desk.

"I left a customer hanging in the shop so I could
sign some forms?" Jeff wasn't yelling. He never yelled.
But his voice was scary calm.

Miss Dickson held up a pen. Shaking his head, Jeff
took it from her and started scrawling out info.

"Why wouldn't you just bring these home, Noah?"
Jeff asked.

I shrugged.

"*Noah.*"

"They all ask the same stuff. And it's not like they
don't already know how to reach you." I arched an eyebrow rather than point out the obvious. They had, after
all, just called him in.

Jeff stared at me for a long time. I could tell, even

though my head was ducked, because Landon stared from me to him, me to him. Landon's dad died in a car crash when his mom was pregnant with Henry. He always acted weird around Jeff, like he was at the zoo, observing monkeys in their somewhat natural habitat. I could almost see the thought bubble over his head: *This is what life is like with a replacement dad.* Now it could be: *This is life when a replacement dad is annoyed.*

Jeff gripped the pen and tackled the forms. I glanced up at him just as he looked over at me, his eyes softening as he figured it out. Every one of those forms—each and every one—asked for Mom's address. For her contact information. And I couldn't do it. I couldn't write Center Regional Jail on those lines. Jeff nodded once at me and silently filled out the papers.

He slid the stack toward Miss Dickson and handed her the pen.

Miss Dickson's mouth puckered at Jeff's oil-stained hands. She grabbed a tissue and plucked the pen from his fingers with it as Jeff's face reddened. I've never hated anyone more than I did Miss Dickson and her stupid bubblegum-pink face at that moment.

She studied the papers. "Is this to be Noah's permanent address?"

Jeff stared at her. "What do you mean?"

"Will Noah be staying at this address for the remainder of the school year?"

Jeff crossed his arms. "If plans change, you'll be the first to know, Miss Dickson." I swallowed as if the words were a pill or something. *If plans change.* Maybe he was just putting Miss Dickson in her place, letting her know she was being nosy. Or maybe Jeff just didn't want to answer. Maybe the plans *would* change when Mom was released. Jeff rolled his shoulders and turned back to me. "Ready, Noah?"

I nodded, shoving my folder and notebook into my backpack. "Remember, just clear the denominator and you're golden," I told Landon.

"Whatever." He turned away from me.

"Landon," Jeff asked, "need a ride home?"

Landon's mom rushed into the lobby just then. "No," she said crisply. "I'll take my son home."

Jeff nodded. "Nice to see you, Abby."

Landon's mom acted like she didn't hear Jeff. Funny, she never had a problem talking with him when Landon needed a ride to football practice last year. Henry, hoisted onto Abby's hip, laid his head on his mom's bony shoulder. Still groggy from his nap, he yawned then pointed a chubby finger toward me. "No-no!"

No-no was Henry's name for me, but Abby must've forgotten that, too, because she just lowered his hand

and said, "Yes, Henry. Landon made a no-no, missing the bus again." Landon didn't respond, just raked his backpack up his shoulder and followed his mother out of the lobby. "And now I'm going to be late for work. Again. Which means another demerit. Two more, Landon, and they're going to fire me, and then what? Have you thought about that?" Landon didn't say anything as he trudged out the door.

Another a memory I didn't want of my own mother slammed me.

It was Mom picking me up in third grade after I socked a kid in the mouth. The kid had pushed me because he wanted my spot in line for the slide. I had told him to go to the back. He tried to push me again. But I blocked it and punched him in the gut. The elementary school principal, a lady who loved the phrase "Hug it out," said punching was never okay, and I had a three-day suspension. Then she called Mom.

In Mom whirled like a tornado. She had been waitressing then, and still wore her apron. She smelled like hoagies and pickles. "What's going on?" She kneeled to look me in the eyes. Her fingers raked across my forehead and under my chin, tilting my face up to hers.

The principal cut in before I could reply, telling Mom that I had punched a boy.

"Noah?" Mom hadn't said it like I was in trouble,

either. Just like she hadn't heard a word from the principal and was still waiting for me to answer.

I never could lie to her, never even wanted to. "I punched him." The principal made a tsking noise with her tongue, but Mom's gaze didn't waver. "He pushed me and was going to do it again."

"Three days suspension," the principal chirped.

Mom nodded, face still soft as pie. "That's my boy. You've got to fight back when someone pushes you around." Mom had stood then, holding my sweaty hand in her cool grip, as the principal waxed on about nonviolent ways to handle conflict. "Save it for the boy who started this. My boy and I are going out for ice cream."

CHAPTER FIVE

The second time I saw the bear was in the middle of the "Bring Back the Bruins" frenzy.

By the end of September, the Bruins Bucket Challenge swept the school. Landon had videoed his challenge and posted it to the school site. Soon there were fifty other kids, drowning themselves in blue, orange, or red drinks by the case. The website couldn't handle the traffic, so Brenna started a "Buckets and Bruins" social media page. It had hundreds of likes the first day.

On the way to school, I stared out the bus window and counted buckets. Seventeen this morning on our route. Landon had ended his video by throwing the bucket over his shoulder. The person filming it—Mike, probably—focused on the bucket in the yard as the last scene. Now that was part of the thing, I guess. Everyone tossed their empty bucket over his shoulder and left it in the grass.

The hallways smelled like Arctic Blast and Lemon-Lime from the kids too lazy or proud to take a real shower after their "challenge." Their sneakers squelched against the tile floors. Walls were sticky from their fingers. Someone in the bathroom moaned that he was stuck to the toilet seat. I think he was joking. Definitely didn't check.

Suddenly Bruins colors—orange and black—filled the school again. Landon wore his jersey almost every day. Brenna wore her old cheerleading uniform, but Mr. Anderson made her wear leggings under the skirt. Sometimes I thought I was the only one who didn't sport Bruins clothes. Even Rina in her all-black, all-the-time attire appeared full of school pride.

Rina had somehow managed to create a newspaper. I mean, I guessed it could be called a newspaper. It was one printed page that she was handing out to everyone as they came into school. Across the top, right under BRUINS GAZETTE, she wrote about the Bringing Back the Bruins fund-raiser, and how just making a big donation to MADD didn't guarantee the League would take us back. I mean, take the team back.

The League is run by a committee comprised of two members from each team in the surrounding area. They would need to vote to reinstate the Bruins, which had been fined $200 following the forfeit of last year's championship game. The donation might be enough of a goodwill gesture, but reinstatement isn't guaranteed.

Next to the article, just over a snippet announcing that "the editor welcomes reporters to apply for a position in the newspaper," was a smaller piece about the fund-raiser itself. The headline was *To Fill or Not to Fill*. Her article stated: *A case of energy drinks costs about $9. To fill a standard-sized cleaning bucket, a person would need to use the entire case. In addition, he or she is then supposed to donate an additional ten dollars to the fund. Wouldn't it make sense to just donate $20?*

Fundraising planners refused to comment.

That last part was surprising. Bringing Back the Bruins seemed to be the only thing anyone wanted to talk about. That and trashing Rina's "newspaper." When Rina tried handing out copies in the hall between classes, Mike whipped most of them out of her hands. Landon then offered to help Rina, but once he gathered up the scattered papers, he dumped them all in the trash can.

Still, a few days later, Rina had her notebook in her hand and pencil at the ready when there was another assembly. This one was held out on the (former) football field, where we sat on still-dewy grass.

The makeshift stage that's usually in the cafeteria/gym/assembly room had been carted out to the middle of the field. Mr. Anderson stood in the center, holding a megaphone instead of a microphone. "Let's go, Bruins!" he called.

The crowd went nuts.

"We love school spirit here at Ashtown Middle

School," Mr. Anderson kicked off. "But the janitorial staff is complaining about the condition of the hallways, desks, and lockers. Bugs are becoming an issue. Anyone who comes into school smelling of energy drinks will be sent home to shower."

A bunch of kids jumped to their feet, complaining. The flurry sent a new wave of sickly sweet energy drink stench across the field.

Mr. Anderson held up his hand for silence. No one listened.

"Knock it off!" boomed the gym teacher and he blasted his whistle. Slowly, everyone simmered down.

"All right. Any questions?" Without even turning toward her, Mr. Anderson sighed and said, "Rina."

Rina popped to her feet in the front row, notebook still in hand. Mike groaned. "Thank you, Mr. Anderson," she said formally. "Rina Beltre of the *Bruins Gazette*. My question is two part. First, exactly how much money has the Bruins Bucket thing raised?"

Mr. Anderson smiled in a grimace-y sort of way. "That's a question for Brenna, but I understand we're nearly at triple digits!"

"It's just that the big poster in the hallway is showing that about fifty dollars—two digits—has been raised."

The Adam's apple in Mr. Anderson's throat bobbed so hard my own throat hurt. "Is that your second question, Rina?"

Her sigh drifted heavily over the field. "No." Her voice raised high so that even I could hear in the back, she continued, "But let's say the poster hasn't been updated and we're nearly at triple digits, aka a hundred dollars. But, by my count, more than fifty people have thrown a bucket over their heads, which means that a minimum of five hundred dollars should've been raised. So the goal would be met and we can stop the fund-raiser. Right?"

Silence from Mr. Anderson.

Silence from the crowd.

"Is it possible that people are forgetting the 'and donate ten dollars' part of the challenge after they dump wasted overpriced energy drinks over their own heads?" Rina continued.

"You can mix the energy drinks with water!" a cheerleader yelled.

Mr. Anderson stared at Rina.

"Shut up!" someone shouted from the middle of the crowd. "Boo!" came from near the goalpost. Soon almost everyone was hissing and booing, some people even throwing balled-up paper—copies of her own newspaper—at Rina. She stood stock-still in the front, notebook still in hand, waiting for Mr. Anderson's reply.

"Now, now," the principal said weakly.

I sat on my fists and bit my lip, swallowing down my own fury. But it bubbled out anyway. "Leave her alone!" After being quiet for so long, I didn't realize how loud I could be. My voice sliced through the buzzing until everyone was quiet again.

"Do you have something you'd like to add, Mr. Brickle?" Mr. Anderson said. I caught a glimpse of Mr. Davies, standing beside the stage. He smirked.

"Yeah." I stood, but kept my head down. Already a paper ball hit my back. "Rina's just asking a question. Back off."

"Sit down, Sneaks, and shut your stupid piehole!" Landon didn't even try to cover up that he was the one yelling.

The room would've erupted again, this time aiming its anger my way, had the bear not appeared.

The blue bear had grown. She was still small but carrying more weight around her middle than last time I had seen her.

She lumbered out of the woods at the edge of the field. The kids in the back saw her first and started screaming. "Bear!"

Mr. Anderson stood on tiptoe at the stage, looking out over the field, yelling into the megaphone for everyone to remain calm. But that totally didn't work. Just about everyone jumped up, pushing the row ahead. Half the kids screamed, the other half laughed. I twisted as I stood, trying to keep an eye on the bear. She faced the woods, her backside toward us. She should've run off, away from the people and the noise. Everything I had heard about bears said they are more afraid of us than we are of them. Yet she didn't move, not coming toward us but not backing away, either. I jumped up onto the stage so I could see her better. Mr. Anderson paced on stage, barking, "Code Yellow! Code Yellow!" into the megaphone as streams of kids ran into the building.

Someone pushed into me, also climbing up onto the stage. Rina. "They shouldn't be running!" she yelled at Mr. Anderson. He lowered the megaphone and pulled out his walkie-talkie, still screaming, "Code Yellow! Code Yellow!"

Rina swiped the megaphone from his hand and called into it, "Everyone! Walk calmly backward from the bear. Don't run! Stop running! You! Stop running! Walk calmly backward from the bear!"

Another crumpled paper ball nailed her in the head. "Seriously!" Rina hissed into the megaphone. "A bear is a few feet from away and you take the time to make a *spitball*? You deserve a mauling!"

"Give me that!" Mr. Anderson grabbed the megaphone and shooed us from the stage. He told Mr. Davies he was going to run ahead and unlock the doors. "Make sure everyone gets inside!" he yelled, and pushed through the crowd.

"Come on," called Mr. Davies, turning Rina around by the shoulder and motioning for me. But then I caught a glimpse of the bear straight on.

"Oh no!" I yelled. By now, just a dozen or so kids were rushing toward the entrance, everyone else pressed against windows inside the building. Each of them skidded to a halt, turning halfway back toward me. I hadn't realized I had yelled so loudly. Again.

Mr. Davies grabbed my T-shirt at the shoulder, pushing me forward. "Come on, Noah, into the building." He put out his arm to herd Rina in, too, but, like mine, her feet were planted.

"Look!" I yelled. "Look at her!" I pushed back against his arm, sidestepping so his grip on my shirt loosened.

Rina strained against Mr. Davies's other outstretched arm. "Is that a—"

"Yeah!" I yelled, taking two strides closer toward the bear. "It's a bucket."

"That's not something you see every day," Rina mused.

The bear now faced us from the other side of the football field. Or rather, she would've faced us. But wedged on her head was a black plastic bucket. Somehow she must've scratched out a hole at the end of it, because I caught a glimpse of her snout.

A strangled, snorting yelp echoed from the bucket.

It brought me to a stop, but just for a second. Just as I started to rush toward her again, two things happened. First, she rushed back into the woods. Second, Mr. Davies tackled me.

The teacher rammed into my back, his arms wrapped around mine, slamming me into the ground and knocking breath from my lungs. I was paralyzed under his weight. His mouth next to my ear, Mr. Davies rasped, "You have to get into the school, now!"

All elbows and shoulders, I scuttled out from under him. I scanned the woods for a trace of the bear. She was gone. Popping back up to my feet, I turned to face Mr. Davies where he now sat, legs out and breathing deeply on the grass. Funny, you'd think he'd been the one tackled.

Behind us, the rest of the kids trickled back into the building. A crowd gathered just inside the doors, but teachers were swarming, pulling students from the door and into the classrooms. The door swung shut with a loud click.

Just Rina stayed, her eyes darting between us and the woods.

Mr. Davies grunted, pushed up with his hands, and stood. "Noah, what were you thinking? Rushing after a . . . " His mouth twisted like Miss Dickson's as he stifled whatever adjective he wanted to use. ". . . bear! Do you have a death wish?" He reached for my shoulder.

I twisted away. "She needs our help! It's stuck on her head."

"What's stuck on whose head?"

"The bear! A freaking bucket is stuck on her head!"

Mr. Davies paused. "Is this a joke to you?"

He again reached for my shoulder, pulling me closer toward him and the doors to the school. I tried to lunge away from him, and Mr. Davies pulled me back again, so hard I tripped. I hung for a second by his hold on the collar of my T-shirt. "Get up!" he said. "We have to get inside!" I planted my feet, but now our faces were just inches apart. I felt all the blood leave my face even as his flushed tomato red. He yelled, "Who do you think you are? Listen, I'm in charge here, not you. Follow my rules. When I say get into the building, guess what?" He shook my shirt in his fist as he said the next words, "You." Shake. "Get." Shake. "In." Shake. "The building!"

I jumped back from him, and the collar of my shirt cut into my neck before ripping.

"I'm glad you're here to see this, too, Mr. Anderson!" Rina's voice was an eerie calm after the science teacher's stormy words. Breathing so hard his nostrils flared, Mr. Davies slowly turned his head toward Rina. She held up her phone, camera facing us. He looked behind him. Mr. Anderson stood there, his face white and mouth open.

Mr. Davies gritted his teeth. "That's out of context. Rina, Noah, time to go inside." He quickly walked toward the building. Mr. Anderson motioned for us to follow, and then locked the door behind us.

Rina took a small step toward me and stopped, her dark eyes even bigger than normal. "You okay?" she mouthed.

I nodded, not knowing why I was trembling. I didn't want her to see me stumble. I swallowed hard and nodded toward her phone. "Good thinking, filming that."

She grinned. "Battery died. Total bluff. I got one shot of the bear, then zilch."

CHAPTER SIX

I thought I'd be called down to the office. All day, I waited for Miss Dickson's gloating voice to float over the intercom. But, by lunch, it still hadn't happened.

So I went down on my own instead.

"Mr. Brickle?" Miss Dickson twisted her lips. "To what do we owe the pleasure?"

"I'd like to see Mr. Anderson." I plunked down into the chair outside Mr. Anderson's office.

"He's unavailable." Twisty lips, twisty lips.

"I'll wait."

"Go to class."

"I have a free period." Like I was proving a point, I pulled a book out of my backpack and laid it across my legs. The words swam across the page but I pretended to read them. Miss Dickson sighed and punched buttons on her phone. She cupped her hand over it and whispered into it. Very subtle, that Miss Dickson.

I was barely through pretending to read a full page when Mr. Anderson stormed into the office, Rina on his heels. The nervousness I had seen earlier—after what happened with Mr. Davies—flickered just a second in his eyes. "Mr. Brickle, I can't deal with you right now."

Rina pushed forward. "Just look!" She waved a paper in the air. "Another A-plus!"

"Congratulations, Rina." Mr. Anderson sidestepped by me.

"Same. Narrative. Essay!"

"Mr. Anderson," I broke in, planting my feet in front of the door to his office. "What are you going to do about the bear?"

He half-turned away from me, only to be inches from Rina.

"Fourth year in a row, Mr. Anderson," she continued. "There is a serious dearth of creative thinking in this school!"

Mr. Anderson sucked in a huge breath, his shoulders pitched with the effort. His eyes darted from Rina back to me. I had never seen my steady principal so close to losing it. Slowly, Rina pulled her phone from her back pocket and oh-so-casually glanced at the screen. She murmured, "I could just upload a video while I wait . . . "

"Come in," Mr. Anderson growled and leaned past me to open the door.

Rina pranced into the room and sat in the far chair. I took the one next to her. "You first." Mr. Anderson nodded toward me. "What's your issue?"

"The bear. What are you going to do about the bear?"

Rina bounced in her seat and pulled the reporter's notebook from her massive backpack.

Without looking up from the stack of papers on his desk, Mr. Anderson said, "We'll be on the lookout for the bear. If it wanders onto the field again, we'll have a Code Yellow and contact the police." He jerked his head toward Rina. "You're up."

"Wait!" I didn't mean for my hand to slam down on his desk. I'm pretty sure my face looked just as surprised as his and Rina's. "I mean, the *bear*. What are you going to do about the bear? To, you know, get the bucket off her head."

Mr. Anderson cocked his head at me, like a dog that heard the word "treat." He leaned back in his office chair with a creak and crossed his arms behind his head. "Why are you so concerned?"

His eyes pinned me in place. I licked my lips, not sure how to answer. Why was I worried about the bear? I glanced over at Rina. Funny, I never noticed her eyes were a dark mix of green and brown. Hazel, I think it's called. Mr. Anderson cleared his throat, and I realized Rina and I were staring a little too long. Rina turned away and studied her notebook.

"I—I don't know." I ducked my head. "It's not right. The bear. It just got stuck in that bucket." I felt my jaw tighten. "It's not its fault. It can't get out."

No one moved for a long moment. When Mr. Anderson picked up his phone and began pushing buttons, I got up from my seat at the dismissal. But Mr. Anderson pointed back to the chair. He cleared his throat again. "Yes, this is James Anderson, principal of Ashtown Middle School. I had called earlier regarding the bear that came onto school grounds today." Pause. "Yes, what will you be doing to help the bear's situation?"

Mr. Anderson listened for a few minutes, thanked the person, and hung up. He turned to me and Rina. Her pen hovered over the pages of her notebook. Mr. Anderson's nostrils flared again for a second. "The Department of Natural Resources is looking into the bear. They've got a rep searching for tracks."

The only sound was Rina's pen scribbling on the pad.

Brick-sized thoughts—apologies, questions, thankyous—crammed into my skull. But none of them traveled down to my mouth.

"Now," Mr. Anderson continued, "back to class."

I pushed up to my feet and walked out just as Rina flipped a page and began asking about changes to the writing classes.

In math, I deduced that the number of shoves in the back is exponentially connected to whether a person stands up for someone opposed to a football fund-raiser.

In science class, I discovered that Mr. Davies was dumber than I had thought. And that's saying something, because I had pegged his intelligence somewhere around sloth. Did you know sometimes sloths mistake their own arms for tree branches and fall to their deaths? Well, Mr. Davies fell nearly as far when he ended a lecture about gender roles in animal species by bringing up football. Funny thing is, I actually agreed with Mr. Davies this time. His lecture wasn't dumb; giving it to this football-loving class was.

"Sports like football, they serve no purpose in today's society. They're as archaic as gladiator games. With any luck, our society will evolve to the point where men can showcase power with intelligence, rather than their ability to hold on to a ball."

For a few seconds, complete silence blanketed the room. I looked up and saw Rina's hands float upward like she was about to start a slow clap. I shook my head quickly at her, and she sat on them instead. Then, the silence crumbled and the booing began.

"Oh, come on!" Mr. Davies burst in. "How does it help kids like you when whole stadiums cheer you for touchdowns but ignore you when you ace a test or treat others with kindness? How awful it must be when the bleachers are quiet."

I kept my eyes locked onto my desktop, trying to push away the noise in my head. The noise of packed bleachers chanting for the Bruins. Mom and Jeff's roars louder than anyone's. The slosh of ice and Gatorade as the coolers were lifted and emptied over my head. My neck suddenly felt heavy, heavier than when I was weighed down with all that gear.

"It's all just posturing," Mr. Davies said over the hissing in the room. "It's setting us up to fall from grace, making boys feel like they belong, only to snatch it away the minute the timer runs out or the team loses."

"So don't lose," Landon called.

"Are you following me?" I felt, rather than saw, Rina standing just behind me at the end of the day.

"Paranoid much? I have the locker next to you."

"Since when?" I blurted.

Rina sighed, deep and heavy. "Since always, oh Master of Observation." She twirled through the combo on her lock and popped open the door next to mine. Photos of Eleanor Roosevelt, Maya Angelou, and—strangely—the two grumpy Muppet men were taped to the inside of her door.

"What?" she snapped when she caught me looking. "I like to accessorize."

"That's such a girl thing to say."

Rina cocked an eyebrow at me. "Did you know that *I* am a girl?" She waved a hand down herself, and my eyes followed across her black T-shirt and dark skinny jeans.

"Well, obviously." And then I felt like an idiot because it really made it sound like I had been checking her out. Which I guess I had been. She was cute, in an annoying, always-smarter-than-you sort of way.

Both of us turned back to our lockers without looking at each other again. The walls on mine were bare.

"You should get a lock, you know." Rina pointed to the heap of trash, none of it mine, in the locker. It had taken me a few days after school started to realize that no one was mistakenly using my locker. They were doing it on purpose. Real clever, right? Kids pointing out that I'm nothing by using my locker as a trash can. I swiped the balled-up copies of Rina's newspaper, a hamburger wrapper, chewed-up gum, broken pencils, and more onto the ground.

"Or you could just create tripping hazards," Rina continued in a superior you're-so-dumb voice. "That'll work, too."

"Who asked you?"

But just as Rina was about to slam shut her locker door, I saw it. A snapshot from last year of her with her arm around Micah. Even though he's twice her size, she was somehow looking down at him. He was smiling hugely into the camera, holding up a Butterfinger candy bar.

Man, he loved those things. It started when Landon gave him one at practice for a laugh. You know, like calling him "Butterfingers" since he could never hold the ball long. But, of course, Micah, who never seemed to learn much past third grade, didn't get the joke. He loved the candy bar, though. Before long, someone always had one for him. It wasn't to be nasty, either; it was because when Micah was happy, you couldn't help but be happy, too. Too quickly the memory switched to the last I had with Micah, with him sprawled on the field. My heart hammered in my chest.

"He's okay, you know?" Rina whispered. "The whole leaving school thing—that was his mom's idea. She was planning it for a long time before . . . Well, it's not your fault. Not really."

I tore my eyes away from the picture.

"You know," she said softly, "Mr. Davies is a complete dunce. But even dunces have a point once in a while."

"What's yours?" I kept my eyes down, knowing I was being a jerk but not being able to stop. Not wanting to hear her next words, but not able to walk away, either.

"Sports being full of posturing. Leading to falls from grace. The rest of the world isn't like it is here. I met all of these kids at camp this summer, kids from all over the place. When you get out of this town, you'll see. Football isn't—"

I threw one of my books into the locker. "Get out of this town?"

"Yeah, when you go to the college or—"

Both of us stopped talking and turned back toward our lockers as Mike and Landon passed. They were throwing a soft, Nerf-style football back and forth. *Just pass by. Just pass by.* But, of course, they didn't. Mike's shoulder rammed me just under my shoulder blade, shoving me into my open locker, my forearms slamming into the sides.

"Watch it!" Rina snarled, but Landon only laughed and threw the ball. Mike scrambled ahead, knocking into a couple of sixth graders to get the ball.

"You might not have to wait that long. For me to leave I mean," I said. "My mom gets out in six weeks."

Rina stilled, her hand on the locker door. "Are you moving when she comes home?"

I shrugged. "I don't know."

"What makes you think you would be?"

"We only moved in with Jeff so I wouldn't go to foster care," I muttered. I wanted to look around and make sure no one was listening in, but if I looked up I'd see Rina's face. So I just stared at the trash heap in front of my locker. "He and Mom were fighting—that night, I mean. A big fight."

"You think they were going to break up?"

I shrugged again. "Jeff's too good a guy to dump her after what happened. He'd feel too guilty. Already feels like it's his fault I was in the car. But when she's out . . . "

She shut her locker door and turned toward me, crossing her arms. "I don't know, Noah. He seems like he really likes being your dad."

"He's not my dad." Jeff was stuck with me, but the countdown was on. Soon he'd be free. It was even written on the calendar, circled in red.

I slammed shut my locker door, so hard that it whipped back open. I slammed it again. And again.

Rina's fingers, light as butterfly feet, landed briefly on my shoulder. I jerked aside. I didn't mean to. I mean, I know she was just being nice. But I guess I'm not used to someone touching me. Jeff isn't the touchy-feely type. Rina started to say, "In a few years, no one will—"

I pushed shut the locker door before she could finish.

CHAPTER SEVEN

I didn't even like football.

That's the thing. I used to be a soccer player.

I had never even touched a football before Mom took me to Jeff's place for the first time. I was eleven then. He was the first boyfriend Mom had introduced to me in years.

Jeff had cooked this big spaghetti dinner and was slipping frozen garlic bread in the oven when we walked in. Watching Mom just open the front door and stroll to the kitchen in the back of the house reminded me that, while it might be my first time there, that wasn't the case for her.

Jeff offered Mom some wine, and I sucked in my breath until she said no thanks. She grabbed a glass from the cabinet and got herself water from the tap instead, winking at me over the top of her glass. She was keeping her promise not to drink again.

"What's with the jersey, kid?" Jeff had asked me.

I shrugged.

"He's obsessed with Leonardo Messi," Mom piped in.

"*Lionel*," Jeff and I corrected at the same time. Jeff smiled at me, eyes crinkling. I wanted to smile back, but I didn't. It was like I wasn't ready to be on his team against Mom, if that makes any sense. Mom opened the kitchen door to the backyard and gave me the go-ahead to head out. The sun had set, making it too dark to really run around. Someone—Jeff, I guess—flipped on the porch light.

I heard them talking inside, voices low, the smell of garlic and sound of Mom's laugh filtering through the screen door.

An old football lay on the grass. The skin was worn off in places, showing white patches of thread. I picked it up and rolled it in my hands a little.

When the screen door creaked open, I turned to see Jeff standing there in the glow of porch light. He held up his hands and jerked his chin toward the ball.

I threw it, but it was more like a fling, the ball landing with a thud by his feet.

"Come on, Messi." He laughed and picked up the ball. Stepping closer to me, he showed me how to hold the ball. "Let it kind of roll off your fingers." Jeff reared back and threw. The football sliced through the air, landing across the yard.

I trotted across the grass and picked it up. Holding it like he had shown me, I threw it back to him. The ball landed in Jeff's hands with soft, satisfying thud. "Not bad, kid." Jeff nodded and smiled. This time I smiled back at him.

Soon we were throwing the ball back and forth, both of us pushing further, making each other dodge and jump. Jeff pointed to a tire he had swinging from a tree branch. "See if you can get it through the middle."

I did, on the second try. Jeff whistled low.

"Boys!" Mom called. "The bread's burning."

"Diane," Jeff said over his shoulder, "you didn't tell me your boy had an arm."

Soon I was heading over to Jeff's place or his shop after school most days. We'd chug milk from the carton and head outside to throw the ball. Sometimes Landon would show up, too—Jeff throwing the ball and the two of us rushing for it. Within a couple weeks, Mom was joke-whining that Jeff only dated her so he could play football with me. But I could see that she was smiling, too. Eventually, Mom had said I had to finish homework before playing ball. So we just ended up always hanging out at Jeff's from after school until bedtime.

Then, one day, Jeff brought home a flier for the Ashtown Bruins Boys' Club Football League.

I made the team.

Coach Abrams made me quarterback.

"Your boy's got a great arm," Coach had told Jeff after tryouts.

★

Miss Peters kept me after class. "You're not working to your full potential, Noah."

I shook my head. "I aced the first test." I wasn't bragging. It was true. I only got one wrong, and no one got it right, not even Rina. In the five weeks since school started, Miss Peters had given two quizzes, and I had aced those, too.

Miss Peters nodded, her ponytail swinging. "You are. But in class you're not sharing your ideas. You know what Mr. Anderson said about good citizenship? Participating is part of being a good citizen."

I felt my stomach boil. How could she talk to me about being a good citizen, when she put me in a group with Brenna and Mike? The two of them couldn't make it clearer that they hated me. Sure, Mike couldn't pull off the same meanness in the classroom that he did in the hall—bumping into me, trashing my locker, calling me names. But, in class, he and Brenna sat with their backs to me, whispering like they thought I was trying to cheat by overhearing them get the problems wrong. I just doodled in my notebook instead.

I gritted my teeth and didn't look at her. Miss Peters held out her hand. "Give me your notebook."

Reluctantly, I handed it over. She flipped to the last page I had open. In between slashes and boxes, there were numbers.

"These are correct. And very, very different from

your small group's conclusions." She pointed to a specific number. "This answer? Twenty-one? That's right. Your group submitted 401. A bit of a difference, wouldn't you say?"

Her fingernails were clipped short, squared at the unpainted tips. I shook my head slightly, thinking of how Mom always kept her nails pointed, long, and painted.

"I broke you up in small groups today so you could problem-solve together, each of you bringing something to the decision-making. There is a reason I put you with Mike and Brenna, Noah. They aren't as confident as you in math. They need a leader, someone who can not only get the answer right, but show them how to reason through it. You could be that leader, Noah."

I pulled the notebook out of Miss Peters's hands and closed it. "I'm going to be late for my next class."

Miss Peters sighed. "Noah, you've got to step up a little. Take some ownership. Don't you want to be a leader?"

My teeth, they were going to crack, I clenched them so hard. But I couldn't grind out the memory.

"You own it out there, man!" Landon's arm slaps across my shoulders. "Go Bruins!"

The rest of the team rushes us, answering Landon's cheer. My fist pumps into air, the cheers from the bleachers washing over me.

"Our MVP . . . Noah Brickle!" Coach Abrams dumps

a cooler of orange Gatorade over my head, my grin so huge I couldn't help but taste it. Coach leans in close, the stubble on his cheeks brushing against my ear as he whispers, "What would we do without you, kid? You're leading this team to the championship. I can feel it!"

Mom clapping so hard, cheering so loud, she's about to fall off the bleacher. Jeff sitting beside her, hands linked behind his head, nodding and smiling like I'm the greatest thing ever. Like he's proud.

"No," I told Miss Peters, "I'm no leader."

"You're wrong, Noah," she called as I walked out. "You're just not ready."

In English comp, Ms. Edwards crossed her thick arms and glared at each of us. "We're adding a new section. Instead of continuing with personal narratives, which *some students* seem to feel is repetitive, we are now going to focus on small moments."

"*Yessss!*" Rina hissed from the front row as everyone else groaned. Rina's hand shot in the air.

Ms. Edwards ignored her. "Write about a time when everything suddenly became clear for you. A moment when you knew what you had to do in order to solve a problem." My mind went blank. Problem-solving isn't exactly a strong suit of mine.

Ms. Edwards's chair creaked as she shifted in her

seat, ignoring Rina's hand waving in the air. But Rina didn't stop, and swung her arm like it was a flag. A squeak bubbled out from her. Ms. Edwards finally took a long breath. "Rina, is there yet another way you'd like to alter my curriculum?"

Rina bounced in her seat. "I was just going to suggest, Ms. Edwards, that our small moments be very different from our personal narratives."

Ms. Edwards glared at Rina over thick glasses.

After English, both Rina and I stopped at our lockers before heading to Mr. Davies's science class. "Congratulations," I said to her.

She grinned, shoving her fluffy hair back into a ponytail. "I know, right! Death to the personal narrative! Onward with the small moment!"

"They're basically the same thing."

Rina slammed shut her locker door. "Nonsense! I have achieved victory!" She peeked over at my locker. "Less trash today."

"Yeah." I rooted around. "I can't find my science folder, though. So, um, is your small moment going to be getting the small moment into the curriculum?"

"Sneaks!" some kid—a sixth grader by the look of him—shouted as he passed by. When I stood up, he scurried down the hall. Great, Landon and Mike's nickname was catching on.

"Nope." Rina's grin stretched further and she kept

on as if the little twerp hadn't said anything. "My small moment was establishing the school newspaper."

I groaned. "You're keeping up with the paper?"

"Yep." Rina leaned in, her hair tickling my ear. "And I'm recruiting writers."

I couldn't help smiling back at her, even though my science folder—which had been in my locker that morning—had vanished. "No way. I have enough of a target on my back."

Rina smiled. "We'll see."

I still was smiling as I went into Mr. Davies's class, though I knew chances were small that he'd believe someone stole my folder out of my locker.

CHAPTER EIGHT

At the end of the day, I took what was becoming my usual seat in front of Miss Dickson's desk in the lobby. "Can I call Jeff? I'll just walk to the Shop."

Miss Dickson twisted her lips and shook her head. "When we have after-school detention, Noah, we wait for a parent or guardian to pick us up. It's in the handbook."

"Yeah, but detention is over. Can't I save him the trip? I walk to the Shop every day after school."

Miss Dickson ignored me.

I threw down my bag on the chair and slumped in the empty seat beside it. Just then, Mr. Anderson came out of his office. "Back again, Mr. Brickle?"

"After-school detention," Miss Dickson broke in. "Seems we can't remember to turn in our science folder."

"Someone took it out of my locker!" My fingernails dug into my palms. I don't know who I was angrier with—Mr. Davies for not believing me, Miss Dickson for her digs about it, or me, for letting both of them bother me.

A buzzer pealed through the office. I looked up at the security camera footage to see Jeff waiting by the door. Miss Dickson pressed the button to open the doors.

"Detention, Noah?" Jeff asked in his low, quiet voice as he strode in. He had circles under his eyes. The rag he used to wash his hands was shoved in his back pocket. I wondered how many customers were left fuming so he could get me this time.

Mr. Anderson crossed his arms and cocked an eyebrow at me. "We were just about to discuss that," he said to Jeff, though his eyes stayed on me.

I opened my fists and flexed my fingers. "Someone has been going into my locker. Trashing it. This time, they took my folder. It was there this morning, with my work in it."

The principal stared at me for a long moment. "Did you share this with Mr. Davies?"

"Yeah." I shrugged. "He doesn't believe me."

"You must have given him some reason to think you'd be something other than truthful."

Jeff cleared his throat. His mouth pressed into a hard line. "Which assignment? The branch diagram of rock life cycle?"

I nodded. For some stupid reason, the corners of my eyes stung. I had covered the small kitchen table with work yesterday. Jeff had sat with his bowl of chili on his lap, asking me questions about how the rock layers illustrated evolution. It had been kind of cool, I guess. Felt like I was teaching him every time he asked a question. After he washed his dishes and went to have a smoke on the porch, I rewrote the assignment, adding in some details Jeff had seemed surprised to learn. I was still working on it when he went to bed.

Now Jeff turned to Mr. Anderson. "My kid, he did the work. And it was good. I looked it over this morning. His folder was in his backpack."

Mr. Anderson didn't say anything for a long moment, letting those two words—*my kid*—bounce around my skull. "I'm afraid I can't intervene without talking with Mr. Davies. I won't undermine one of my teachers."

Jeff made a *humpf* noise the same time I did. "Come on, Noah." Jeff opened the door for me. "We free to go?" he asked Miss Dickson.

"He served his time, so yes." She put a wrinkled hand to her bubblegum mouth. "Oh! Didn't mean to offend."

"Of course not," Jeff replied, his voice steady.

When we got to the truck, Jeff sat shaking his head, staring ahead toward school. I jumped when he slammed his hands into the steering wheel.

"I'm sorry," I muttered.

Jeff mopped his hand across his face. "Noah, don't."

He shoved the key into the ignition, grinding the gears a second. "I'll get you a lock."

Right as Jeff shifted back into drive, I grabbed the wheel. "Hold it!" I yelled.

Jeff slammed on the brake.

"Look!" I pointed to the patch of woods across from the school. "There! Do you see her?" I unbuckled and ran from the truck before Jeff put the car in park. I heard his footsteps thud onto the blacktop just behind me.

His hand curled around my elbow, locking me in place, as the bear stepped out of the woods, thrashing her head back and forth. She was about forty feet in front of us, the bucket still pinned around her head. She rose a little on her back legs and slammed down on her front, then shook her head again.

"She knows we're here," Jeff said in a low voice, right into my ear. "But she can't see us."

"We have to help her!"

The bear backed up at the sound, then turned and ran back through the woods.

"Come on!" I pulled away from Jeff, but his grip tightened.

"And do what, Noah?" He dropped his hold on me and raked his hands through his hair. "She's not going to let us get near her. Even if she did, do you really think we're going to get close enough to pull that thing off her head? And that she'd just thank us and be on her way?"

Something about Jeff's calm reasoning ignited me. I stepped backward from him. "So we do nothing? We just let her live like that?"

Jeff moved closer to me. "No, man. We call the authorities."

"Like who?" I looked around, like someone would appear. "We're the only ones here."

"The people in charge. The people whose job it is to take care of animals. We have to trust that they'll do it."

A sound—I guess it was sort of a growl—ripped out of me. "Yeah, cause that helps! It's been days. She's got to be suffering!" I wanted to throw something, punch someone, destroy anything. But the only person in front of me was Jeff.

He took another step toward me, slowly, like I was the wild animal. "Maybe the people in your life, the ones who should be taking care of you, aren't doing a knockout job. But, Noah, you're a kid. This—" He gestured toward the woods where the bear had disappeared. "This isn't your job. It isn't your doing."

Jeff's soft, cautious words punched the air from my lungs. I shook my head, fast. "This isn't about me!" My voice cracked on the last word. And then I was crying, like a stupid baby. Bending my legs and ducking my head and pulling my hair and crying.

Jeff's arms wrapped me. I clutched myself harder, not leaning into him at all, but he didn't let go.

A long time later, or maybe it was just a few minutes, we made our way back to the truck. The doors still hung open. Jeff bent to pick up the keys from where he had flung them onto the pavement. We sat in the cab without talking. Jeff scrolled through a page on his phone and called the animal control number, being transferred again and again, until he talked with someone about the bear. "Yeah," he said. "A bucket, wedged on its head." Pause. "Yes. I said bucket. *Bucket*."

And it wasn't funny. But it was funny, hearing it like that. I couldn't help it, I laughed into my fist. And then the corner of Jeff's mouth twitched and he made a choking sound into the phone. "Yes, officer, I know. It's no laughing matter." He hung up and we were holding our stomachs and letting our chuckles fill the cab.

"It is kind of ridiculous, I guess," I said.

"You know," Jeff said, "I *have* noticed a ton of buckets in people's yards on the way to the Shop."

"It's this 'Bring Back the Bruins' thing, with people dumping energy drinks on their heads." Soon I was telling Jeff all about the fund-raiser, about Brenna and Landon, about the trash in my locker, about Rina getting her small moment. All of it came tumbling out, Jeff nodding as I spilled, maybe asking a question here or laughing at something there. When I told him about Landon shutting me out, he pressed his mouth together, but didn't say anything.

"I guess," I kind of muttered, "this bear's problem is my fault."

"How do you figure that?" Jeff asked, an edge to his voice.

I shrugged. "The buckets are part of raising money for the football league. And I'm the reason it . . . "

Jeff sighed. "Bit of a stretch, don't you think?"

I didn't answer, just told him about Rina's newspaper goals.

Next thing I knew, the sun was setting and we were still driving around in the truck. "Hey, you missed the turn," I said as Jeff drove right past the Shop.

He laughed. "Dude, we've driven pass the Shop about sixteen times. Glen's not even bothering to wave anymore."

"Why'd you do that?" I felt my face flame.

"I like talking to you, Noah. Didn't want you to stop." Softer, he added, "My dad, he used to just let me talk, too."

I sucked on my bottom lip, suddenly not having anything more to say.

CHAPTER NINE

I glanced behind me the next morning, as buses lurched to a stop and kids streamed into the school. No one looked over here at the edge of the woods. Quick as I could, I unzipped my backpack and pulled out a plastic grocery bag. I dumped the contents at the edge of the woods and darted back toward school, cramming the empty bag back in my backpack and hoping the bear found the apples and hunks of beef jerky before any other animals did.

Maybe Jeff thought it wasn't my fault the bear was trapped, but I knew the truth. None of this would've happened if it weren't for me.

"Noah!" Miss Dickson singsonged as I entered school that Friday. The sea of kids parted, giving me nowhere to duck. "Mr. Anderson wants to see us in the office!"

"Already?" I sighed.

"Maybe it's something good," Rina piped in. I hadn't realized she was just behind me.

"Whatever." I pushed through the office door, Rina still on my heels.

"Relax." She smiled. "I'm not following you. I just have my own business with Mr. Anderson."

"You realize you willingly go to the principal's office almost as often as I'm forced to do it, right? I think you have some sort of sickness."

Rina grinned, flashing her white teeth and crinkling her hazel eyes. "I'm wearing him down. Mom said I can't make all of the newspaper copies on her printer any more—too much of an environmental impact." She rolled her eyes. "So Mr. Anderson is going to give me carte blanche to the teachers lounge and its mega copier." She crossed her arms and popped up her chin, taking long strides toward the principal's office.

"Carte blanche?" I repeated.

"It means blank check." Rina shrugged.

"You know, maybe more kids would read your newspaper if you used words they could read."

Rina paused and I bumped into her from behind. She turned around, her mouth puckered like Landon when he tries to solve math equations in his head. "Good point. You're going to be an awesome reporter."

I laughed. "Yeah. No way."

Mr. Anderson's shoulders rose almost to his ears; that's how big his sigh was when he saw us. "Rina." He twisted his neck back and forth like he was prepping to spar. "You might as well hear this, too, since you won't stop pestering me about it." Rina grabbed her reporter's notebook from the front pocket of her backpack and flipped to a new page. She glanced over at me and wiggled her eyebrows in a told-you-so sort of way.

Turning toward me, Mr. Anderson continued, "Your bear was spotted a handful of times over the past few days. I called the Department of Natural Resources again this morning. They haven't caught it yet, but they're making progress. Thought you'd like to know."

I felt the corner of my mouth pop up. "Thank you!" The words sounded funny in this room. Mr. Anderson nodded. He seemed to have a hard time fighting a smile, too. He cleared his throat. "But listen, if I hear from the janitorial staff that you've been putting food in the woods again, you're in serious trouble. Suspension trouble."

I squirmed. I didn't think anyone had seen me. "It was just a couple apples. Some beef jerky."

Mr. Anderson narrowed his eyes. "Don't feed the bear, Noah."

Landon brought the soft football to school again, tossing it in the hall to Mike, who passed it to someone else, on and on. I blended into the crowd after leaving the office, watching out of the corner of my eye as the ball sailed back and forth across the stream of students.

"Go, Bruins!" someone shouted, and soon everyone was chanting. "*Bru*ins! *Bru*ins! *Bru*ins!"

Before football games last year, this is what every Friday was like. Funny how my heart hammered faster, keeping beat with the chant. Like it didn't know it wasn't part of the team anymore. Like there was a team.

I saw the ball sailing toward me. Everything in me knew not to catch that ball. Everything but my hands, I guess. I caught it, pulling it in to my chest. Suddenly the chant stopped and the hall quieted. It was just me and the ball. *Drop it,* I ordered my hands. *Drop it and walk away.* Stupid hands didn't listen.

The bell rang, the hall emptied, and I still held that stupid football. When teachers closed doors and I knew I was late, I still couldn't drop the ball. At the end of the hall was a big, black trash can. Could I still do it? Could I still make the shot?

Stupid hands took over. I reared back and let loose, the ball twirling as it slid in a graceful arc, sinking right into the middle of the open trash can. Stupid mouth smiled.

I whipped around, ready to hustle to English comp, and smacked into Landon. His face was twisted and red. "The trash, Sneaks?" He shoved me with two hands, and I landed with a thud at his feet. "I hate you."

It didn't hurt. Not really. I mean, my tailbone sort of throbbed where I hit the tiled floor, but it wasn't a real hurt. I could've bounced right back up. But I didn't. I stayed there, eyes closed, listening to the squelch of Landon's sneakers against the floor as he rushed the trash can to get back his ball (or maybe just to put distance between the two of us).

When I couldn't hear him anymore, I opened my eyes. Back on my feet, I walked the wrong direction and headed toward the nurse instead. The last time I had been there was for the obligatory vision test at the end of last year. I don't get sick much. But she knew me. "Noah," she said, looking up from her computer screen. "Your face is flushed. Are you feeling all right?"

I shook my head, and she gestured to a cot. I lay on it and closed my eyes.

A few seconds later, I felt her cool fingers on my forehead. "You don't have a fever," she murmured. "Does your stomach hurt?"

I nodded, even though it didn't.

"Well, you rest a bit, okay?" She pulled shut the curtain around the cot.

Rest. That sounded good, a caramel to melt slowly on my tongue.

But I couldn't. I rolled onto my side and squeezed shut my eyes. All I saw was the bear, thrashing out of the woods. I flopped to my back. I smelled lavender, and I closed my eyes to picture Mom leaning in to whisper a story in my ear. But that made my stomach boil more, so I rolled onto my other side, and somehow heard Landon's steps moving farther away from me.

Finally, I spit out the soured idea of rest all together.

I lay back on my back and stared at the thick ceiling tiles. A piece of green grass was wedged between the grating holding up the drop tiles. How could that have happened?

I bit my lip, hard, when a baby whimper leaked out of my mouth.

"I'm sorry, Noah," the nurse called out from behind the curtain. "Do you want me to call your . . . your guardian?"

I shook my head, forgetting for a moment about the curtain, then mustered out, "No, thank you."

I was tired—too tired to push away memories. So I didn't. I let myself remember. The scenes came in flashes. Once I let in the first, the rest lined up, vying for their chance.

First, tryouts. I had thought Jeff would drop me off, but he parked instead, hanging out by the fence and watching Coach Abrams put us through the drills. When it was my turn to throw, I glanced over at Jeff. He pushed off the fence, standing straight. He winked at me and nodded. I let the ball rip from my hands. Coach Abrams whistled, long and low, and slapped his hand on my shoulder. "Quite an arm you've got there, Brickle."

Next up, celebrating after the first game. Mom, Jeff, and I went to Sal's Pizza. We were going to get a pizza to go, head home, and watch a movie. But Landon and his mom, Mike and his folks, even Brenna and a couple other cheerleaders, filled up the restaurant. They called my name as we entered, Landon pushing us to stay. Mom shared a booth with Landon's mom, talking about how they'd get the grass stains and mud out of our uniforms.

Coach Abrams sat next to Jeff. Everyone was laughing. The fifteen million different conversations zipped around and over us but somehow included us, too. Abby filled a glass of beer from a pitcher and handed it to Mom. She winked at me and took a tiny sip. I shook my head at her and Mom pushed the glass away. Micah, his uniform spotless, came in with his mom. In that full throttle way of his, he fell into the seat across from me. "Good game, guys!" Micah said. Landon high-fived him and elbowed me under the table to do the same. An hour later, Mom's glass was empty. She sang a little too loud as Jeff drove us home, but in the morning she was drinking coffee and smiling, so it wasn't like before, when it was just the two of us and she used to drink.

A flash of the scoreboard. Bruins ahead by twelve in our third game of the season. Coach Abrams put his arm around Micah. "Head in and have some fun, kiddo," he said. Coach winked at me. By now I knew what it meant: let Micah play. Coach only put Micah in when we knew we'd win. The bigger kid's hands and feet didn't work like the rest of ours. He'd stumble over his cleats. Even the other team always seemed to sense it, no one tackling him even though he was the biggest target. I tossed a light ball his way.

Another flash, this one of me and Jeff eating at his kitchen table. Mom was in the living room with a bunch of other moms, having a booster club meeting, talking about how to raise money for better bleachers. "Enough of this!" Brenna's mom called out. "Let's go have a drink at Sal's." Mom shot a look our way, and Jeff smiled and nodded back. "I'll give you a lift home," he whispered when she pecked his cheek on the way out the door. I thought about telling Jeff about *before*, about when Mom used to get in trouble. About how that's why Mom doesn't talk to her family anymore. About how I used to dump bottles of liquor down the drain when she was in the shower. But I didn't say anything. Mom winked at me. "Just one glass of wine," she promised.

My heart thudded faster, wanting the memories to stop there. But they kept running.

The playoff game now. Just one image: Landon in front of the end zone, arms up. The ball leaving my fingers from across the field, arcing like an arrow straight into his open hands. The touchdown. The scoreboard. The team, rushing me. The splash as Coach Abrams dumped the bucket over my head. The cheering. Jeff's grin. Mom's rosy cheeks. "My boy," she said, again and again. "My boy."

My rabbit heart thumped harder now. My stomach churned. I curled onto my side, trying to stop what comes next. But I couldn't.

Mom coming home, face shining, thrusting a huge shoe box toward me. I tore it open to see candy-apple-red sneakers, brand name. "Just in case you weren't cool enough." Mom laughed. "An early Christmas present!"

Coach Abrams's party—the night before the championship game. Jeff promised to meet us there; he had to close the Shop first. Mom ruffled my hair and told me to sit up front next to her in her car. Coach Abrams hugged me when we arrived. The other moms, standing around the kitchen island, cheered for Mom, and held up their wine glasses. Landon and I, and the rest of the guys, threw the ball in the backyard. Jeff's truck pulled up much later. He waved at me on his way into the house. A few minutes later, he was guiding Mom to the car. She pushed him away, telling him he's no fun, her words slurring.

Jeff slammed the truck door shut and pulled away alone. Other people left, trickling out one by one.

Mom leaned in the doorway. Landon's mom invited

me to spend the night at their house. "No," Mom, eyes too bright, words melting into each other. "My boy's coming home with me." Mom dropped her keys. She smelled sickly sweet. Drunk, just like *before*.

In the nurse's office, I whimpered again. But the flashes wouldn't stop.

The stop sign, a blur of red on the right. Lights, too fast, too close. My hands pulled the wheel, jerking it right. Mom's scream was shrill. A siren pierced the night behind us.

Blue lights flashing in the side mirror. "Don't tell them, Noah!" Mom crying. "Don't tell them I'm drunk." An officer barked at me to stay in the car, to keep my hands up.

Mom, in handcuffs.

Mom being pushed into the back seat of the cruiser.

Mom! Mom! Mom!

In the nurse's office, my stomach boiled. Heart hammered. I felt sweat bead on my forehead even though my arms were covered in gooseflesh. The nurse pulled back the curtain. "You seem peaked," she murmured. "I'm calling your guardian."

I shook my head, but couldn't scatter the images.

"All right," she said. "I've never seen anyone fight this hard to tough out a day of seventh grade. But since you're not feverish or actively throwing up, I can't make you leave. Just rest for another few minutes."

I couldn't leave now. Not when the worst memory had finally pushed to the front of the line. It flashed like an explosion.

The championship game, the next morning.

The game, just me and the ball and my team. Touchdown after touchdown. Fury flooded me again and again, despite the score.

The countdown. Two quarters left. One quarter. Five minutes. Three. When the time ran out, that'd be it. The game would be over. Season over. And what would I have left?

Coach Abrams gave Micah the go-ahead to head out. "Simple Pitch play."

I took the snap. Tossed the ball to Micah. And he just stood there. Doing nothing. *Nothing.*

So I rushed him.

Hit him with my shoulder.

Absorbed the crunch as the defensive tackle rammed Micah into me.

Heard his strangled cry but ripped the ball free from his fingers anyway.

Ran to the end zone.

Scored the touchdown.

Heard how loud silence can be.

And me, alone.

"Noah?" the nurse asked. "Are you ready to go back to class?"

I nodded, still staring at the ceiling. "I'm feeling better now," I said, even though my whole body wanted to sleep.

The nurse frowned down at me. "Why don't you rest a little more, Noah?"

I must've fallen asleep right away. The light was different in the room when I woke. As the nurse left to write my excuse back to class, I stood on the cot and nabbed the stray piece of grass wedged in the tile.

CHAPTER TEN

Coach Abrams used to make us watch video of games. We'd go through each and every move. "You don't know what to do next until you know what you've already done," he used to say.

Funny how lying there in the nurse's office, watching the play-by-play of my life, helped me form a plan.

I couldn't change anything. I had messed up a lot. If Mom and Jeff stayed together once she was out, that was up to them. I couldn't change it and I hadn't made it easier, considering the times Jeff had to come pick me up at school. So Jeff was either going to let me stay or kick out me and Mom next month. I'd still have to face Mom eventually. The Bringing Back the Bruins thing wasn't going away, and wasn't going to push the spotlight off of me.

But I could, maybe, change something.

Maybe I could save the bear.

"Hey," I said to Rina, who stood by the lockers at the

end of the day. She jumped about six inches off the ground and dropped a book onto her foot.

"Ow, ow, ow!" She jumped on one leg. "What are you thinking, scaring people like that?"

"First of all," I said as I bent to pick up her book, "it was a simple 'hey,' not 'boo.' Secondly, you did the same thing to me this morning. Third, what are you doing carrying around such a massive tome?"

Rina cocked an eyebrow. "Tome?"

I shrugged, feeling my face heat. How could I tell her that being around her made me want to sound smart? Luckily, she smiled. "It's *Grimm's Fairy Tales*, the complete collection."

"It's the size of a cinder block."

"Hence the *complete* part." She grabbed it from me, our fingers brushing, and zipped it into her backpack. I had this crazy urge to grab the bag from her and carry it instead. Not because she was weak or anything. Just because I didn't like the idea of it cutting into her shoulder.

So, of course, I said something dumb. "Aren't you a little too old for fairy tales?"

Rina sighed. I didn't need to look up from shoving my own books into my backpack to know she threw an eye roll in there, too. "Did you know there's a fairy tale in here about a girl whose dad makes a mistake and she ends up having her hands chopped off by the devil? Doubt Disney's going to make a movie about that."

A snorty laugh slipped out at that. Very smooth.

"So what's up, Noah?" Rina crossed her arms and stared at me.

"Uh, nothing." I closed my locker door.

"Come on." She sighed again. "You're so full of crap. One day you don't talk to me at all, the next you're using words like 'tome' and being all gentlemanly."

"Maybe I'm just a nice guy."

Rina's hand floated toward me, like she was going to touch my arm. I didn't mean to, but I sucked in my breath. Her hand fell to her side. "I know you're a nice guy, Noah." She cocked her eyebrow at me again. "What do you want?"

I swallowed hard, not knowing where to start. "It's just. There's this thing. And I was wondering . . . I mean, you know how to . . . "

The bell rang. "Are you taking the bus today?" Rina asked.

I shook my head. "I'm heading to Jeff's shop."

"Cool. I'll meet you there in a half hour. Maybe you'll be able to string words into sentences by then."

As soon as I got outside the school, I looked up the Department of Natural Resources on my phone. I cleared my throat and dialed. It was dumb to be ner-vous. I mean, it was just a phone call, right?

"Department of Natural Resources, how may I direct your call?" the person on the other end said and I almost hung up.

But instead, I croaked out, "Yeah, um. I'm calling about a bear."

"Okay," the person said. "Where is the bear now?"

"Um. I don't know," I said, suddenly feeling super stupid. I didn't even know how to make a phone call. I cleared my throat again. "It's the bear, the one with the, um, bucket on its head."

"Oh, right. Bucket Bear. I'll connect you with Ron, the officer handling that case. I can give you his direct line, in case you're disconnected."

"Cool," I said. "Hang on." Quickly I pulled a scrap of paper and a pencil from my backpack. Holding the phone wedged against my ear, I copied down the num-ber and then was transferred.

"Officer Ron speaking. What's your issue?"

The warm, cozy feeling from the first part of the call vanished. Officer Ron had a voice like he guzzled rocks for breakfast—deep and gravely. I cleared my throat again. "Yeah, I'm calling to see if you've caught the bear yet."

"The one with the bucket on its head?" I heard crin-kling sounds, probably a wrapper being rolled up and tossed in the trash. "The bear is still at large."

"Any spottings?"

The officer sighed. "No. These things take time. Give me time." More munching sounds came through the line.

And suddenly I stopped being nervous and just was annoyed. Couldn't he wait until he was off the phone? How seriously was taking the bear if he could eat a Tastykake through talking about her?

"Yeah, I'm sure you're real busy and all."

Officer Ron's voice deepened even more. "I'm heading out now to check the traps. All right?"

"Yes, thanks," I said. "I'll give you a call tomorrow."

"These things take time," he said again.

"Right. I'll call you tomorrow."

"What's your name, kid?"

"Noah. Noah Brickle."

"All right, Noah Brickle. How about you let the grown-ups handle this?"

"I'll call you tomorrow, sir."

Officer Ron sighed as I hung up.

As soon as the call ended, I ran to the Shop, waved to Glen and Jeff, then cleaned off the counter. I even fed the vending machine a few quarters for a couple pops and bags of chips. Of course, Rina probably only ate organic juice and free-range tortillas or something like that. I worked through the words in my head until they actually were sentences. I'd play off calling the DNR as

no big deal. Like I had loads of experience calling gov-
ernment offices. But the first time I tried to talk, it was
to Jeff, and I still stumbled.

"I'm, uh . . . A friend is meeting me here. For a project. I mean, to start a project. Maybe a project."

Jeff and Glen stood behind a laptop, ordering parts.
Glen pursed his lips and chewed on his cigarette. Jeff
crossed his arms and stared at me, his mouth twitch-
ing. "A project, huh?" he said.

"This *project* . . . " Glen rolled the cigarette along his
mouth. "It involve a girl?"

"No!" I snapped. "Well, the friend, she's a girl. But
the project isn't a girl."

"*Uh-huh*," Glen and Jeff said, in unison.

"It's not a big deal!" I flung my arm out, accidentally
toppling a tin can full of screws. I caught it, shoving the
screws back inside, and elbowed another can, this one
full of pens. "It's just a thing."

"Sure," they said.

"Seriously, guys!" I stumbled backwards. "It's not
like that."

"This *thing* . . . " Glen chuckled. "She cute?"

"What? No! I mean..."

"Oh, she's cute," said Jeff, rolling onto his toes and
looking behind me into the shop lobby.

I whipped around just as Rina turned toward us.
She stopped and raised an eyebrow at the way we were

all staring at her. I waved and she tilted her head a little but kept walking. "Just shut up about it," I hissed as they laughed.

I led Rina toward the workstation. She dumped her backpack onto the counter and ripped into the bag of sour cream and onion chips. "Awesome! I'm starving." She gulped down half the can of pop. "So, what's up?"

"Um." I sank onto the stool next to hers. "It's just…"

Rina rolled her eyes again. "Spit it out, Noah. What do you need help with?"

"What makes you think I need help?"

She stared at me, chewing on her chips.

"It's the bear," I finally said, hating the way my voice cracked on *bear*.

"Bucket Bear?"

I shrugged. "Yeah, if you have to call her that."

"What's wrong with 'Bucket Bear'? I mean, it is a bear with a bucket on its head."

"It's a little more than that, don't you think? I mean, just calling her Bucket Bear is sort of callous."

"Hans Christian Andersen calls a girl who is literally starving and freezing to death the "Little Match Girl" because she has a match. I think a bear with a bucket on its head can handle being called Bucket Bear."

"Okay, fine," I said. "Whatever. This bear—"

"Bucket Bear."

"Yes, that one. Can we move on?" I waited until Rina nodded, not liking how she wasn't even trying not to grin. "So Mr. Anderson called the Department of Natural Resources this morning, right? Well, I called again after school. They still haven't caught her."

"Yeah." Rina nodded. "I called, too."

"You—what?"

"I called." She pointed to the other bag of chips. "You gonna eat those?" I pushed them toward her. "My mom is health freak. She'd probably force me to eat baked, non-GMO, free-range tortilla chips if they were a thing." Rina shoved a handful of barbecue chips in her mouth. "So, yeah, I gave them a call after school, too. No wonder the guy seemed so annoyed. You must've just gotten off the phone with him."

"I get the impression Officer Ron is generally annoyed," I said. Rina smirked. "But why did you call?"

Rina licked some barbecue powder off her fingertips. "Look, since school started, you've reacted to absolutely nothing. Nada. Not teachers picking on you. Not trash piling in your locker. Not your best friend death glaring you across the cafeteria. Then this bear shows up and suddenly you care about something again. It didn't take a genius to figure that's what this," she pointed between us, "is about. Which I am, by the way. A genius, that is."

"Congratulations. It's just . . ."

Rina shrugged. "It's genetics. I can't really accept the congrats on brainpower I was born having. But I assumed that's why you wanted to talk to me. Because I'm smart, like you. And I know how to get things done." She smiled into the distance, no doubt thinking of her small moments English comp win, totally ignoring the fact that an additional task on the curriculum list made her about as popular as me.

"It's just . . . "

"There are more than 250,000 words in the English language. If you say, 'It's just,' one more time—"

"I want to save her," I blurted. "The authorities aren't doing a good job."

"I agree."

"They're setting live traps, but I bet they can't get her to them because she can't sniff them out. And black bears are super fast, too, so they can't catch her."

"So what can we do?" she asked.

"I'm not sure." I opened the laptop Jeff had loaned me and typed *black bear* in the search engine. Rina leaned over my shoulder, not speaking but reading along as I researched. I could tell she finished reading pages before me, but she didn't say anything about it, just leaned back in her seat until I was finished.

Once she reached around me and clicked on a story I would've skipped since it wasn't a science or environmental page. It was a news article from a couple weeks back, about a huge black bear that had been hit by a tractor trailer. I swallowed as I read. My bear was so small, and she practically had blinders on, thanks to the bucket.

After a few minutes and a half dozen web pages, Rina said, "Okay, so what do we know, aside from that the bear doesn't have a lot of time?"

"Well, that first site said bears should be hunting and eating like crazy this time of year to bulk up for hibernation. But she can't do that because of the bucket, so she's probably not eating nearly as much as she should."

"Yeah," Rina added, "but at least something else makes sense now. I couldn't get how she was even still living. We first saw her like this a week ago."

"But that natural resources site had a lot of info about hibernating and— "

"Right," Rina said. "Everyone always thinks hibernation is about it being super cold. But it's not. Hibernation is from lack of food, not winter. So maybe she's going in a pseudo-hibernation? Pseudo means fake."

"I know what pseudo means."

Rina grinned, like she was proud of me. Man, she could be irritating. But, for some reason, I smiled back. "Right. But it's dangerous, because right now she should be eating a ton of food, building up her fat stores to get through actual hibernation."

"So even if we save her, it might not be enough?" Rina asked.

"Maybe not." I gritted my teeth. "But I want to give it a shot."

"What can we do?" Rina asked.

"I think we should track her. You know, the more people we have looking for her, the better. Maybe we could do search parties or something."

Rina's mouth twisted. At the same time, Jeff bellowed, "Hell, no."

"Jeff!" I yelled, annoyed that he was listening.

"No way," he said, his voice firm. "No way are a bunch of kids going tracking through the woods after a scared, desperate bear. No way."

"Look," Rina broke in when I opened my mouth to protest. "Your dad's right."

"He's not my dad." I kept my eyes down so I wouldn't see Jeff.

"Even so, he's right. We can't go looking for the bear ourselves. But what if we got other people to do it?" She smiled. "You know why this 'Bring Back the Bruins' bucket thing is working, even if it isn't raising as much money as it should?"

I shrugged and turned away from Rina, putting my elbows on the counter. I didn't want to talk about the bucket contest.

"Because Landon, Mike, and Brenna got people to

care about it. That's all. Whether it's successful at raising money or not, it got people to talk about the football team like it's a real thing again. And that's why it's
going to work. If you want to save Bucket Bear, we've
got to get people to care about her."

"How am I going to do that?"

"Well, you already got me to care." Rina put her
elbows on the table, too, so our arms touched. I felt a
buzz, like soft electricity ran along that length of skin.
"And that was just by mumbling incoherently."

"No one's going to care what I have to say."

"Dude, enough with the pity party." Rina crumpled
her chip bags and tossed them into the trash can. She
missed. "But I agree with you. You do have a bit of a
reputation problem. People have long memories."

"Exactly!" I slammed my fist on the countertop.

"So we've got to get people to care without knowing
they're caring about *you*." Rina messed around with the
laptop, then flipped it so it faced me. "Check this out."

This time, I rolled my eyes. "Yeah, I've heard of
social media." Rina had a half dozen sites gridded
on her screen—Twitter, Tumblr, Reddit, Instagram,
Facebook, Snapchat.

She pushed a few more buttons and the screen just
showed a picture of the bear. "This is the only shot I
got during that assembly before my phone died. But
maybe it'll be enough." She chewed her lip a second.

"We make the bear go viral. Get people to upload when and where they spot her."

"Maybe add Officer Ron's contact info, too. So he'll know right away?"

"Save the Bucket Bear!" Rina cheered, like Brenna. Then she turned to me and was back to being know-it-all Rina. "Social media presence is huge, according to my dad. He says that's what sells books these days more than anything. And at my journalism camp, the editor said digital copy is gold. What do you think?"

"I think you're a genius," I whispered.

"We've covered that already." But she smiled.

"Looks like the *project* is going well," Glen said from behind us.

"It's amazing," I said, not taking my eyes off Rina.

Her fingers flew across the keyboard, setting up sites. "Can we add a map thing?" I asked. "So, like, people can check in where they see her."

Rina nodded.

"And they'll be able to post pictures, too, right?"

She smiled. "I like where your head's at." We went over setting up passwords and monitoring. She made me administrator of each site, and I jotted down the details.

"This is incredible," I said an hour later, when all the sites were live. "Thank you."

"Oh, you don't have to thank me." Rina stowed her

notebook back into her shoulder bag. "You have to owe me."

"Owe you? What?"

"You," Rina poked me in the chest, "just became the first reporter of the *Bruins Gazette*. Welcome to the newspaper club, Noah. I'd like an opinion piece on saving Bucket Bear by Tuesday."

"But I thought we were keeping my reputation separate from the bear?"

Rina shrugged. "We'll try to use it, too. See which sticks."

"Which sticks?" I groaned.

"Yeah. Think about it. Every time a celebrity does something stupid, they get all over the news. Then whatever movie or project they're working on is news, too. You already did something stupid. Now we make Bucket Bear news."

"I still wish you'd stop calling her that."

Rina laughed and brought her bag back up her shoulder. "Bucket Bear is going to be huge." Then she looked at her watch and sighed. "I've put it off long enough. Time to go home for dinner." Her face scrunched up. "Mom's on this vegan kick. Bean curd drumsticks with roasted kale on tonight's menu. Have you ever bitten into bean curd?" She shuddered.

"Nah, we're more SpaghettiOs and takeout."

"You. Are. So. Lucky," whispered Rina, hazel eyes wide.

"Hey, Rina," Jeff called out from the bay behind us. "Would you like to stick around for dinner? We're just getting burgers from Sal's, but you're welcome to join us."

"Praise the Lord!" Rina clapped. "Let me just text my mom." She danced a little while punching out the message on her cell, and then sat back down. "This will give us time to talk about your first feature. I was thinking a profile of Brenna. A real get-to-know-you piece about what matters to her."

I felt the blood leave my face. Rina laughed—a deep, honeyed laugh that I had never heard from her before—and pushed my shoulder. "Dude, I like you too much to subject you to that."

I laughed with her. A few seconds later, her phone pinged. She glanced at it, frowned and swallowed hard. She cleared her throat. "Um, it looks like…"

"Let me guess: your mom said no."

Rina opened her mouth to deny it, then closed it again and nodded. "Micah's my cousin, Noah. And my mom was at that party—"

"Whatever."

"No problem, Rina," Jeff said from under the car. "Another time."

Jeff insisted that I sit with him at the kitchen table to eat our burgers. "Here, have my pickle." He flipped it into my Styrofoam takeout container, right on top of my fries.

"I don't want a pickle." I tossed it back onto his plate.

"Just eat the freaking pickle, Noah," Jeff snapped. He tossed it back. "It's the only vegetable on the table. I want you to have it."

I picked it up and took a huge bite. "Happy?"

He didn't answer. Both of us kept glancing at the glowing green numbers on the oven clock. Six forty-five. Jeff not-so-subtly knocked the huge stack of letters between us on the table. There were about a dozen of them, all from Mom to me. All unopened. The basket on the floor held about fifty more. I pushed the letters aside, then piled fries on top of the burger patty and smooshed it all together with the top of the bun.

Jeff cocked an eyebrow at me then glanced down at his own burger. He had done the same, only with sweet potato fries.

Both of us reached for the hot sauce at the same time. "Go ahead," he said, and I put five shakes on the remaining fries before handing the bottle to him so he could do the same. Six fifty.

I sucked up the last few dregs of my pop and polished off the burger. Six fifty-eight.

"Noah," Jeff said warningly. "Come on, man."

Instead of answering, I pushed off my seat. Six fifty-nine. I held up the pickle. "Look!" I said, like it was a peace offering and finished it just as the phone rang.

"Noah!" Jeff called, but I was out of the door before the last ring.

Fifteen minutes, that's how long I had to hang out in the backyard.

See, prisoners are only allowed to make phone calls a couple times a week. Mom was up to three calls weekly, now that she had finished parenting lessons, was going to group meetings for addicts, and was meeting with Dean Trenton, her sponsor, every week. And she could only make them at seven o'clock in the evening. Sundays, Tuesdays, Thursdays. Here's another prisoner rule: phone calls automatically disconnect after fifteen minutes.

"Hey, Diane," I heard Jeff say into the receiver. "No, sorry. He's not here."

I stomped further into the yard, tripping over something in the dark.

"You know I'm trying. I am." Jeff paused. When he spoke again, his voice was hard. "I can't force the kid—"

I reached around in the overgrown grass and fallen leaves, trying to see what I had stumbled over.

"When you're back, it'll be different," he snapped. "For all of us . . . I didn't mean that."

My fingers flew back like I had touched a flame when I realized what was there, under all the debris. My old football.

CHAPTER ELEVEN

The next morning, I leaned back against my locker, waiting for Rina. When she finally approached—chugging from a Starbucks travel mug (seriously)—I sort of lost my mind for a second and jumped to my feet. A bunch of kids turned toward me, mouths surprised little circles. All the heat in the world slammed my face, and I knew I looked the exact opposite of Jeff's always-cool-and-steady. But Rina just smiled. "I know, right?" she said, like our conversation was a minute ago, instead of twelve hours earlier.

"One hundred likes on Facebook already," I gushed like a baby. "And did you see the comments?"

Rina nodded, transferring her books into the locker. "Everyone wants to save Bucket Bear! Someone even posted another pic." She cradled the mug in her neck. I grabbed it as it started to slip.

"I can't believe your mom lets you drink this stuff." I sniffed the coffee. "Blech."

"She doesn't know." Rina grabbed the cup from me

and took another long pull. "What did the DNR officer say this morning?"

I fought the smile tugging my lips, happy that she just took it for granted that I called again today. I had a little script that I wrote out in the notes of my phone, to keep from getting off track when I checked in. (Why couldn't Officer Ron just text?) *This is Noah Brickle, calling about the Bucket Bear. I'd like an update on the case, please.* Ron had cut me off this morning. "Yeah, yeah, I know who you are."

I gave up on not smiling as I answered Rina. "Ron said no action on the traps. When I ticked off the sightings people posted online, he said he'd head out and see if the traps need to be moved around."

"Great!" Rina closed her locker just as I worked to pop mine open. "I'll follow up this afternoon."

Both of us sighed as a wave of granola wrappers, empty plastic bottles, and balls of paper rolled out of my locker. "I really need to get that lock."

Rina patted my shoulder. "The good news is, we're having our first newspaper meeting at lunch. In the cafeteria."

"How in the world could that be considered *good* news?"

"You get to have lunch with me." Rina grinned.

"Are your, um, other friends going to wonder where we are?"

Rina rolled her eyes. "You know perfectly well that I don't have any other friends, Noah. Apparently it sounds," she made quote marks with her fingers, "*snobby* and *annoying* to talk about the city."

"Huh."

Rina shrugged. "It's not a big deal. I'm moving in with my dad when I'm in high school."

"What?" I felt like I'd been sucker punched. High school was two years away, but Rina was the only person here who treated me like I was human. I sucked on my bottom lip. On the other hand, Rina definitely didn't belong in Ashtown.

"It's not for certain, but Dad's working on it." She slung her backpack up her shoulder. "So... the cafeteria? I have the table by the library entrance."

"Yeah, I know where you sit." Why couldn't I have just said okay? Now my face was turning red, and Rina was suddenly intent on a hangnail.

"Great," she said.

"Great," I echoed.

"So, okay. I'll see you later, cub."

"Cub?" I growled.

Rina shrugged. "It's newspaper speak for 'new reporter.' You don't like it?"

"No," I grunted. "I do not like it."

Rina sipped her coffee. "Fine. I'll stick with Noah."

As she walked away, I had to admit that, yeah,

having lunch with her might be better than resuming my usual seat alone next to the trash cans in the cafeteria.

People stared and whispered for the first minute or two that I sat with Rina at lunch, but then they lost interest. Rina had a lot of ideas for what do add to the newspaper—different features she wanted and interviews she thought we should do.

"How are you going to fit all of these on one page?" I asked.

Rina smiled. "We'll have to make more pages. I'm *this close*"—she inched her forefinger and thumb together—"to getting Miss Peters to agree to be our adviser. Then Mr. Anderson would have to make the *Gazette* a true school club—"

"And you'd get carte blanche to use more paper."

Rina tilted her head at me.

"Carte blanche. It means blank check," I said, making her laugh.

CHAPTER TWELVE

That Monday, I got to life science just before the bell, since I stopped by the library to check the sites for Bucket Bear sightings. Internet is shoddy at Jeff's house and I had spent most of the weekend cleaning up the yard and helping out at the Shop, so I hadn't been able to check on her sightings. On Saturday, someone had posted a pic of her a half block away from Jeff's house. The photo was blurry, but she was clearly still stuck. The bucket was dented all around. Another person wrote that they had chased her, wanting to yank the bucket off her head, but she ran too fast. Black bears can run up to thirty miles per hour, even with something jammed on their head. Rina told me she had seen a sign with "Save the Bucket Bear!" on a telephone pole. She posted the pic to Tumblr.

I wrote down the names and areas sighted for when I called the DNR later that day. Ron didn't seem to enjoy our calls any more than I liked hearing he still hadn't saved the bear. "We're getting closer, Noah," he had grumbled that morning. "Yesterday we caught a female and cub in the live trap behind the school."

"How is that getting closer?"

"It's a bear, isn't it?" Ron had snapped.

So I barely made it to class on time, something Mr. Davies was sure to notice. I slipped in the door, and quickly saw I didn't have to sweat it. The entire class, including Mr. Davies, was crowded around the windows.

"What's going on?" I asked, leaning around Rina to see what the big deal was. Her hair tickled my nose. It smelled like spearmint.

"It's Bucket Bear!" Rina pointed toward the tree line, where a DNR officer squatted. "She was through here earlier. The officer's looking for tracks."

He must've found some, too, since he got out a camera and snapped a few pictures. "How do they know the tracks are for the right bear?" Brenna asked, in a bored voice. "You know, there are other bears in the world."

"They estimated how old Bucket Bear is based on its size in the pictures people have posted. It clues them in about how big her prints should be. That, and she's been sighted hanging around here." Everyone turned toward me.

"I didn't know he could talk!" I heard a new kid whisper to Landon, who rolled his eyes.

"All right, all right, class." Mr. Davies clapped his hands together. "Back to your seats."

Mr. Davies droned on and on about natural selection. "So when a species' phenotype, or observable trait, gives that organism an advantage, it's going to flourish. Negative phenotypes will diminish." But no one paid attention; everyone's eyes kept going back to the window, like Bucket Bear would come charging through the woods any second.

"Guys, guys!" Mr. Davies snapped. "This is a cornerstone of biology! Pay attention! Right now, I'm observing that looking out the window is a negative phenotype that will lead to this particular species of students failing their next quiz!"

A few people chuckled. I rested my head on my fist, so the view of the window was covered. "Natural selection explains adaptation," Mr. Davies continued, and started talking about karyotypes and chromosomes. I wrote the date at the top of my notebook—October 12—and tried to take notes, but too late realized I was sketching Bucket Bear in my notebook. Too late because Mr. Davies's shadow covered the drawing.

"Fine." Mr. Davies slapped his hands against his thighs. "Let's talk about this bear." The classroom buzzed, kids shifting in their seats and goofing off. I glanced over at Landon. He slumped in his seat, twirling a pen around in his fingers, not looking at anyone.

"Did you see the signs around town?" Brenna asked. "'Save the Bucket Bear?' You don't think they're going to confuse people who want to do the 'Bring Back the Bruins' challenge?"

Rina's sigh cut across the room.

"So this bear." Mr. Davies's booming voice dampened the buzzing. "If this isn't an example of natural selection, I don't know what is." He smirked across the room at us, eyes catching mine. "Anyone hear about the Darwin Awards?"

Rina whipped around in her seat to face me. She shook her head slightly, like she was warning me not to do something.

"Anyone?" Mr. Davies asked again.

Landon half-raised his hand but didn't wait to be called on before saying, "Aren't they given to people who die in stupid ways? Like being too stupid to live?"

"Right!" Mr. Davies clapped. "If we believe that natural selection allows us to weed out those traits that make us weaker, the awards are a way to thank the people who have improved our chances by not breeding." He laughed, a mean *huh, huh, huh.*

"Oh, I've heard about this!" Mike said from the back of the room. "Like the guy who got into a fender bender while picking his nose, jamming his finger through his brain."

A few more laughs sprang out across the room. Mr. Davies, his face shiny as my red sneakers, pointed to Mike and nodded. "Exactly!"

"The editors gave one to a boy who buckled himself to a shopping cart and then had his friends launch the cart with him in it into a lake." Mr. Davies chuckled and shook his head.

"Is it, like, an actual award? Because the people are dead . . . so it probably doesn't mean much to them," Brenna mused. Rina sighed again.

Mr. Davies ignored her. "Another one went to a teenager who climbed the fence of a tiger enclosure to pet the pretty kitty." *Huh, huh, huh.*

"That sounds more like a mental illness at work than stupidity. I mean, is this whole topic even appropriate?" Rina asked. She was booed from a dozen directions.

"What's this got to do with the bear?" Landon's deep voice quieted the anti-Rina movement.

"Everything!" Mr. Davies threw out his arms. "Here we've got a bear so stupid it shoves its head into a bucket. Think about the *effort* at play there, to wedge that on its head so deep. Now it's tromping through the woods, away from anyone who might be able to help it. If that isn't a sequence of genes that shouldn't multiply, I don't know what is."

"Shut up." I said it softly, but he heard. Everyone heard.

"Excuse me?" Mr. Davies asked. His eyes narrowed.

"It's not the bear's fault," I mumbled.

Huh, huh, huh. "Who else could be to blame, Noah?"

My words squeezed through gritted teeth. "We took over their habitat, didn't we?"

Mr. Davies crossed his arms and nodded, glaring at me but smirking at the same time. "Yes, we did. But adaptation should have them fearing humans. Not approaching us."

"But sometimes they can't help it," Rina spouted out. "Just last month, a huge bear was run over by a tractor trailer. She was probably running from one human when she got smacked by another!"

"Maybe," Mr. Davies said. "Or maybe she failed to adapt to her surroundings, so nature took its course."

"I think you have a terrible idea of what nature is all about."

"Who is the science teacher here, Rina?"

"Isn't your degree in teaching social studies?"

Mr. Davies ignored her. "Animals who adapt survive. Animals whose instincts kick in and keep them from us flourish. Those who don't, don't."

"Even if we're the stupid ones who leave buckets filled with sugary drinks in our backyards? I mean, we practically baited her," I spit out.

The new kid's jaw dropped.

Mr. Davies cocked an eyebrow and motioned for me to continue, even as the room rocked with boos.

I felt something in my chest ignite, and soon I erupted. "You really think that this whole stupid thing of filling a bucket with sugary water and then tossing it in a yard isn't baiting them? I read about bears. They have the best sense of smell in the world. Why wouldn't they go after a quick meal? Isn't that adapting?"

"Adapting? To what?"

"To us! To us being stupid enough to think something like that is a good idea!"

"Did you just— Did you just call the Bruins bucket fund-raiser *stupid*?" Brenna gasped, her overly glossy mouth a perfect *O*.

Again, Rina shook her head at me.

"Yes!" I stormed. "Of course it's stupid. It's about the dumbest thing I've ever heard of! Dumping a bucket of Gatorade over your head like you just did something awesome, made some great save! Like it means anything!"

"Just what are you saying, Noah?" asked Mr. Davies, still smirking at me.

I realized I was standing. I waited for the lava to stop gushing up and out of me, but I couldn't stop it. "I'm saying it's our fault. We made the mistake! We should pay for it! Not her!"

"Not who?"

"Not the bear!" Who else could I mean? "We can't bait them and then let them suffer!"

"So you're blaming this not on an animal's stupidity but on . . . efforts to bring back the Bruins?" Mr. Davies said.

"Yes!" I yelled, realizing too late that I was the one being baited.

"And your solution?"

"I don't have one," I blurted. "I mean, who cares? It's just a stupid football team."

Everyone was freaking about bringing back the Bruins, but that's not what they wanted, not really. Brenna wanted the identity she had as a cheerleader. Landon wanted to see the crowds and feel like he had a family. I wanted to be part of something. But a fundraiser and donation to MADD wasn't going change what happened. It wouldn't turn back time and make *our* team again. November fifth was about three weeks away, and whether they filled up that bucket with a big donation or not, whether Mom came home or not, nothing would ever be the same. My mouth opened and closed to put these thoughts into words, but nothing came out.

Landon stood up so fast his seat fell over. He rushed me, nose half an inch from mine. He didn't say anything, just glared at me so I felt his hate stronger than my anger.

"Back to your seats, boys," Mr. Davies said.

Landon backed up, still facing me but a few inches farther away. Mr. Davies nodded at Landon, and then turned his back to us, erasing notes from the whiteboard.

"Let it go, Noah," Rina said softly. "It's not worth it."

"You're right," I whispered back to her. Here's the thing: I knew what Rina meant. The argument wasn't worth it. Trying to make my point wasn't worth it.

But I also knew what Landon heard. That she was saying the Bruins weren't worth it. That the time before the championship game—before Mom drinking again, before Micah falling—wasn't worth fighting for.

"You're going to pay for this," he hissed.

I couldn't help it. I laughed. Didn't he know I already was paying for it? Every. Single. Day.

And then Landon slammed into me.

The two of us flew backward, and I couldn't brace for the fall with my hands since my arms were wrapped around Landon. We smashed into the edge of the desk behind me, my back taking the brunt of the impact just below my shoulder blade. I pushed back against Landon, and maybe it was just the momentum from the shove or maybe he threw himself into me again, this time pulling us to the side. He hook punched me in the ribs, his knuckles cracking into my ribs just under where I had hit the desk. I fell with a thud against the back wall, Landon's knees smacking down to the take the impact, so when I hit the ground, he hovered over me, his face twisted and eyes streaming.

Mr. Davies's hand clamped on Landon's shoulder,

yanking him backward and to his feet. "What is going on here?"

Around us, the class was silent, mouths hanging open. Everything happened so fast no one had even had time to get out their phones, though a few were doing that now. I wiped at my face with my forearms, then planted my palms against the ground to hoist myself up. My back seized, but I kept my face smooth. "I slipped," I said.

"You slipped?" Mr. Davies's mouth hung open and he shook his head. "You expect me to believe that?"

I nodded. Mr. Davies's head swiveled to Landon. "And you?"

"I, uh, tried to catch him." Landon's chin popped upward. He rubbed at his fist with his other hand.

Mr. Davies shook his head again and looked to the class. Everyone had the same something-crazy-just-happened look on their faces—eyes wide, mouths hovering somewhere between a smile and a grimace, cheeks pink. Everyone except Rina, whose head was bowed over her seat, her hair masking her face. But I could see her trembling, her shoulders quaking and her hands clenched under her desk.

"Can anyone back up that this was just a slip?" Mr. Davies called out. "That in the few seconds it took me to erase notes from the whiteboard, Noah Brickle slipped backward, taking Landon with him?"

"Why do you do that?" I cut in. "Always use my first and last name, but only use Landon's first."

Mr. Davies's face flushed. "Is that relevant?"

"I think so." I crossed my arms, even though it hurt like crazy to move my arms. "How come Landon gets to be on a first-name basis and I'm always 'Noah Brickle' or 'Mr. Brickle'?"

Mr. Davies tilted his head, then shook it again the way a dog would to get rid of a fly. "It's a sign of respect."

"Is it?" I repeated. Funny thing, after Landon slammed into me, all the fury filling me spilled out and away. Yet now, all that spewed-out fury pulled back, gathering like pieces of liquid metal to a magnet, pooling together and back up through my toes and up my legs. Even though I wanted to slump, even though I wanted to rub at my ribs or rest on that cot in the nurse's office, I walked steadily to my desk. I straightened it. We must've hit that, too, when I *slipped*. I lowered into the seat, keeping my face straight and smooth. Landon stared at me. I jerked my chin toward his empty seat. Still rubbing his fist, Landon slumped into his seat.

Mr. Davies shook his head again. All around us, kids picked up their pencils and straightened. I knew it was to protect Landon, not me, but I was grateful anyway.

"Okay," Mr. Davies said after a long pause. "Phenotypes . . ."

★

"What's going on?" Jeff asked that night.

"Nothing." I chewed the last bite of my grilled cheese and took my empty bowl of tomato soup to the sink.

"Then why are you walking around like an old man?" He shook a cigarette out of the box, getting ready to go to the back yard for a smoke.

"Why do you go outside to smoke? It's your house," I said, trying to distract him.

"Because it's your house, too."

"For now," I muttered.

"What?"

"It's my house for now," I repeated louder.

"Noah, what are you talking about?"

I thought of the Shop calendar, the x's crossing out half of October. Two more weeks until Jeff would flip the page to November. Four more days after that and everything would change. *FREE!* "What's going to happen when Mom gets out?"

Jeff rubbed at the stumble on his chin with his knuckles. "Well, we'll bring her home."

I stared at him, not saying anything, but feeling, for a second, like I was flying through the air again, about to slam into the wall.

"And we'll figure out what's next, together." Jeff rolled the cigarette between his fingers. "Listen, Noah, I'm not going anywhere."

I smirked, feeling like Mr. Davies for a second. Maybe he wasn't going anywhere, but were we—me and Mom? Where were we going? When she got out, she'd be in charge again. It'd be up to Mom to decide what I did and where I went, even though she had checked out on me. I swallowed. He didn't know what was going to happen, either. He couldn't promise me.

I turned my back to him, reaching up to grab his lighter from the top of the fridge. I wanted him to know it was stupid, these halfway attempts at being a parent, like smoking outside and hiding the lighter. But instead, I accidentally showed him a couple inches of my back as my shirt pulled up.

"What the hell!" Jeff was at my side in a second, the forgotten cigarette rolling across the floor. He lifted up my T-shirt. I twisted, looking over my shoulder, seeing the dark bluish-black bruises snaking across my back.

"It's nothing." I handed him the lighter.

"Noah." Jeff's voice was scary calm. "This isn't nothing. What happened?"

"I slipped in science class. Fell against a desk. And a chair. No big deal." What was the point of telling Jeff what happened? He'd just feel sorry for me. Or disappointed.

Jeff stared at me for a long minute. Then he picked up the phone.

"What are you doing?"

"Calling the school." He punched in the numbers from memory. "Science class?" he asked me as he dialed. "So Mr. Davies?" I heard the recorded voice of Mr. Anderson guiding Jeff through making a staff selection and focused on that instead of the rush of emotion that Jeff not only had the school number memorized, he also knew exactly who my science teacher was.

I glanced at the oven clock. It was almost seven. No way would Mr. Davies still be there. But he was.

"Yes, this is Jeff Convey. My kid, Noah Brickle, is in your class."

I heard a murmur of Mr. Davies's voice, but couldn't make out the words.

Jeff, his eyes still on my face, continued. "He says he slipped in your class today. There are bruises all over my boy's back. Can you fill me in on what happened?"

Long pause. Why couldn't he have put it on speakerphone?

"That's it?"

Longer pause.

"I'm sure I can count on you not turning your back on your students in the future, right? . . . Yeah. Good night." Jeff ended the call. He shook his head and then handed it to me to hang back on the receiver. His eyes locked on mine.

"Well?" I asked.

"He says you slipped. That one minute you were fine, the next you were on the floor."

I bent over and picked up the discarded cigarette. I handed it to him with the lighter. "See?" I said.

The phone rang, and I picked it up without thinking. Without looking at the time. "Hey," I said into the receiver.

There was a sharp intake of breath, followed by a wobbly, "Noah?"

"Mom," I breathed. My hand clenched the phone so tightly I thought I might crush it. For a second, my eyes closed and I pictured her. Wild dark hair, wide green eyes, pale round face.

Then her words came in a rush. "Noah! I'm so glad to hear your voice! I love you, Noah. I miss—"

I shoved the phone at Jeff and stormed outside. Again without thinking, I grabbed the football and threw it across the yard.

CHAPTER THIRTEEN

had a newspaper meeting before school with Rina. She had texted me a half dozen times last night, promising we'd have a mock-up of the issue to review. It seemed pretty official for something that was going to be just one page. The last text from her was at ten thirty: *Waiting for your column. C'mon, Noah!*

A half hour later, I emailed her a finished column, detailing why I thought saving Bucket Bear was important.

It was strange how fast the words flew out of me. I had spent the whole week dodging writing it for Rina, not sure I wanted to be part of the newspaper at all. But I guessed maybe the whole time I had been kind of writing, too, stringing the words I wanted together in my head even if they weren't on the page. So when I finally opened my notebook, words poured out onto it. I typed up what I had written and then shared the doc with Rina before I could chicken out. I thought I'd get a text from her in a couple seconds, they way she had been hounding me all night.

But total silence from Rina.

The silent treatment seemed to be an epidemic around me.

Jeff dropped me off at seven thirty, on his way to the Shop. We hadn't spoken since Mom called last night. As in, not a single word. Even when I sat across from him at the kitchen table, chomping on Frosted Flakes, he kept silent, sipping his coffee. Even when I yelped a little as I sat down in the truck, when my backpack slammed against my bruises. Nothing.

When he pulled up beside school, he put the car in park and still said nothing. I opened the door and hopped out. "Bye."

He nodded at me. "Hey, Noah," he said as I was about to shut the door.

"Yeah?"

"Ms. Jacobs saw a bunch of food, looked like our leftovers, behind the yard this morning. Know anything about it?" Jeff's eyes zeroed in on mine. "She says a bunch of raccoons were noshing on them. She had to shoo them off with one of her high heels."

"Ah, you know Ms. Jacobs," I said, "always looking for any excuse to talk to you."

Ms. Jacobs, who lived across the street from Jeff, was constantly asking me to call her Cathy because "Ms. Jacobs sounds so old." She and Mom would have coffee once in a while, but lately Ms. Jacobs was always heading out to her car just as Jeff was going to the truck, asking for help changing light bulbs or opening jars, lips glossy and shirt tight. There hasn't been a Mr. Jacobs for a long time.

I ducked out of the car as Jeff laughed.

"Noah." He grabbed my sleeve. "You're not trying to feed that bear, are you?"

"What?" I shook free. I knew it was a stupid idea, but if the food somehow made it to the bear—if I was able to give her some more time—it'd be worth a couple raccoons. "Look, I've got to go. Going to be late."

I didn't look back, just made my way to the library.

Rina already was in there, bouncing in her seat, when I arrived. "Your column, Noah."

"I know. It sucked." I slouched in the seat across from her, only looking up when she didn't answer for a full minute.

"No, no. It's . . . it's incredible."

She pushed out the chair beside her and turned the laptop so I could see the layout of the newspaper. "It really is great, Noah," she said. "But we need, like, five more lines." She pointed to a gap of white at the end of the column. "Is there anything you can add?"

I winced when I bent over to get my notebook out of my backpack. "Let me check my notes. Maybe there's something."

Rina grabbed the notebook. "Let *me* check your

notes. You read over the newspaper. You're our only copy editor."

"I thought I was a reporter."

"Columnist, reporter, copy editor, layout assistant." Rina flipped open the notebook.

"It's in the back," I said.

I read over the whole newspaper. Across the top was an update by Rina on the "Bring Back the Bruins" challenge, including a table with the funds raised. (So far: three hundred dollars.) The article included a paragraph (she called it a "graf") about why the team fell apart. For about five minutes, my stupid heart hammered too hard to read, the words slamming each other around the page. Then I could finally see what she wrote: *Following the arrest of a football player's mother for drunken driving as she left a party hosted by the coach, and the increase of violence on the field, Coach Abrams resigned. The League opted not to hire a new coach or include Ashtown in its rankings. The aim of the "Bring Back the Bruins" is to show the League that the yearlong hiatus has been long enough and the team is ready to play again.*

I made Rina change "hiatus" to "break" but didn't make any other changes. What she wrote fit the principles of journalism she kept preaching about. It was relevant. And it was true.

Rina had written another story—she called it an exposé—on the cafeteria's "price gauging" of berry-flavored seltzer water, which ran along two columns on the bottom left side of the paper.

My column on saving the bear ran along the right side. I hated that my picture was in a little box, but Rina said all columnists need to have a headshot. She can make up rules like that, I guess, since she's editor. So there was my mug, right next to the article about bringing back the Bruins. Rina didn't change much about what I wrote. She highlighted the first sentence in this graf: *When we make a mess, we shouldn't expect others to clean it up. We're the ones who messed up the bear. We need to help her.*

"Find anything I can add?" I asked, my fingers over the keyboard ready to add to the column.

Rina bit her lip and nodded. She flipped the notebook toward me so I could see the page she had open. It was the stupid sketch of the bear that I had made during science class, just before Landon pummeled me. The bucket wasn't on the bear in the drawing, her face was a halo of black pen slashes. The bear's eyes weren't right, either.

"No." I shook my head. "First, it's terrible. Second, she looks too angry. No one would want to help her."

Rina shook her head. For some reason, her mouth was wobbly, like she couldn't form the right words. She pressed her lips together, then said, "She doesn't look angry. She looks …"

"The eyes are messed up. They don't look right."

Rina's mouth twitched again.

"What?"

She shrugged, not looking at me.

"*Rina.*"

"Her eyes look . . . like yours." Rina's cheeks were pink. "I like them."

I swallowed and tried to grab the notebook out of Rina's hand. She tugged it back, twisting to put the notebook down on the table out of my reach. She snapped a picture of it with her phone, then pulled the laptop toward her. A minute later, my bear drawing was sitting at the bottom of the column, my words floating around it.

"I don't get a say in this?"

"Nope." She smiled. I didn't smile back. Rina's eyes held mine. "When does your mom get out, Noah?"

I didn't answer.

A couple hours later, when I was called down to the office, I figured it was because Mr. Anderson found out about the newspaper.

But a police officer was in his office.

My legs froze for a second a few steps outside the room. I felt panic—cold and drowning—pour through me. And then I rushed into the room. "My mom? Is she okay?" I blurted.

"How the hell would I know?" the officer asked. As soon as I heard his annoyed voice I knew this wasn't a police officer. I mentally cussed at myself for being so dumb. This was Ron, from the Department of Natural Resources, not a police officer.

"Noah," Mr. Anderson said, his voice low, "I'm sorry. I didn't think—"

"Nah, it's okay. I'm sorry," I mumbled, feeling all that cold panic morph and burn my cheeks with shame, especially once I saw Rina biting her lip where she sat in the other chair.

"Nice to see you in person, Ron," I said.

But Ron just glared at me as I stared at him. I guess neither of us was too happy with what we saw. Ron was short—maybe about my mom's height—and wide. His eyebrows curled in one continuous, grayish-black line across his forehead. His cheeks were red and chapped, probably from spending too much time outside without sunscreen or any other protection. His hands, crossed at his chest, seemed too large for his body.

"Wait! Are you here because you found the bear?" I asked him in a rush.

Ron nodded as he sank into the seat across from Mr. Anderson's desk. "Yep."

Everything I had been carrying, all the worry I had held on to since I first had seen her, melted away. The

BETH VRABEL   153

bear was free! But then Ron kept talking and all the
worry chilled me again.

"She got away. Spotted her on my way here. Been
watching that Facebook site and monitoring her movement. Good work with that, kids."

"Thank you," Rina said while I jumped out of my
skin for him to continue.

"Anyways, I trekked through the woods and saw
her, all right. She was brushing the bucket against a tree
trunk, trying to knock it loose. Didn't work. I spooked
her, and she took off."

"Why didn't you chase her?" I asked.

Ron just tilted his chin toward me and then looked
down to his wide middle.

Rina scribbled notes into her reporter's notebook.
"How did she seem?"

Ron shrugged. "Skinny. Too skinny. Winter's right
around the corner. Not much time left for her, I'd
guess. It's been, what? Almost a month?" He said all of
this with the same mildly annoyed expression.

"That's it? Not much time left? What else are you
going to do?" I stormed.

"I'm going to ask you to back off, kid. All of you."
He turned and glared at each of us in turn, even Mr.
Anderson. "This isn't the only issue we've got to deal
with, you know. We've got a rabid fox over in Windsor.
Bobcat sightings in people's backyards. Groundhogs

charging on dogs. Fisher cats killing house cats. This ain't the only thing going on. Plenty of other animals need attention, and all we're doing is fielding calls about a stinkin' Bucket Bear."

Ron rubbed at his face with calloused hands. He stared at his lap a second while the rest of us searched for words. This guy, he could out-sigh even Rina. The air seemed to seep out from every part of him. "Look, kid," he said, "I get it. I'm in this business because I like saving animals. This bear, I want it to live. But this is the time animals about to hibernate should be packing on the pounds. Even if we do get the darn bucket off of it, who's to say it's going to survive? It's so small. Its own mother seems to have given up on it."

My teeth gnashed while I chewed over his words. Rina pushed her seat back so it was a couple inches closer to me. She leaned back, her hair pouring over her chair. I felt her watching me but didn't look toward her. Still facing me, she asked Ron, "Does it have a chance? If we do get to her in the next couple of days, does she have a chance?"

Ron sighed again, a little softer. "Yes."

Mr. Anderson said, "But her time is limited?"

Again Ron said, "Yes."

"All right then." Mr. Anderson rolled back on his wheeled office chair and stood up. "Thank you for stopping by, officer."

All three of our heads swiveled toward the principal. "What do you mean, 'all right'?" I stormed as Ron awkwardly stood up.

"So you'll leave me alone, then?" Ron asked at the same time.

The fire inside flamed higher when Mr. Anderson smiled. Then he winked at me! Now I was blazing, a wildfire roaring inside. Just when I was about to explode, Mr. Anderson continued, facing Ron. "What I mean is, while your time is limited, the bear's is even more so. And so we'll be checking in with you four times a day now."

Rina nodded, also standing. "And I'll double the posts online. Anything we get, I'll forward to you directly."

"I'll call you tonight," I promised Ron as his sigh pelted us. He threw up his arms and stomped out of the office.

Mr. Anderson clapped his hands together once. "Great. Back to class, kids."

Once, when I was a little twerp, I found a pack of matches.

Mom had been dating this jerk who was my best buddy when she was around. But the second she left the house, he'd shove me outside and tell me to get lost.

I was too scared to really go far. The only playground nearby was at the primary school where I was in first grade, about five blocks away. I knew I'd get kidnapped like Mom had always warned me about if I tried to go on my own. But this guy—I think his name was Brad—locked the door and wouldn't let me back in the house.

So I poked around the house, peeking into the windows I could reach. I think maybe that was the first time I felt trapped, even though I was on the outside and he was the one locked inside. For sure, it was the first time I felt fury, white and consuming.

I felt it all over again, just thinking about that moment I spotted Brad, sprawled across the couch, eating mac and cheese (*my* mac and cheese!) and watching cartoons in my living room. After peeking through two *SpongeBobs* and half a *Price Is Right*, I gave up on Brad having a sudden wave of pity and letting me back inside my own house.

Instead, I poked around the backyard, looking for anything I could use to jimmy the lock. I found the pack of matches instead. It took a few tries, but I lit one. The boiling egg smell and smoke quickly gave way to an orange flame that snaked too fast down to my fingertips. I dropped it and lit another one. Then another. The color stuck behind my eyelids after the flame died. I saw it with my eyes shut. This, the fire in my hand, it doused that fury inside just a little. Just enough to

breathe. Just enough to make me not think of Brad
(and *my* mac and cheese).

I wanted to make the flames last longer, so I poked
around some more. I found a newspaper in the mail-
box. I twisted it into a torch I could hold in my hand
and held a lit match to it. Just the edges fizzled for a
second, then the newspaper flamed. I squealed and
dropped it, and it danced a bit and then—*whoosh!* The
newspaper was nothing more than orange and reds.
I went to touch it, to put out those flames with my
own hands, when someone grabbed me from behind,
dumping me behind her.

"Noah! Stop!" Mom stomped out the flames. (And
kicked out Brad a few minutes later.)

But all of that, it was nothing.

My opinion piece in the *Bruins Gazette* ignited fury
faster than matches to that old newspaper.

CHAPTER FOURTEEN

I popped open my locker at the end of the day and enough *Gazettes* poured out to cover my feet. Rina picked one up. "Well, at least they're reading." She smoothed the paper out on her locker. "*And embellishing.*"

Someone had drawn round ears on my photograph, plus added something around my neck that looked like those cones dogs have to wear when they won't stop biting their butts. I guess it was supposed to be a bucket. On another issue, a person had sketched a huge arrow piercing into the bear's side, and added a puddle of red ink blood around her body. I gathered an armload of the newspapers and dumped them in the trash can. Rina trailed me.

"Cleaning up your mess, Sneaks?" Mike boomed as he walked by. He slammed his hand down on the pile of papers in my arms, scattering them across the floor. He laughed and kicked them down the hall.

"How bad was it?" asked Rina, helping me to gather them back up. "Class, I mean."

I rolled my eyes. In math, Miss Peters had called on Brenna to make up a math word problem for the class.

Her response: "If five bears get buckets stuck on their heads, how many times will Noah cry and/or blame it on the football team?"

In science, Mr. Davies once again had focused on the Darwin Awards, writing "TSTL" across the whiteboard. Underneath, he added "To Stupid To Live." The only highlight was Rina cocking an eyebrow at me, and I knew she also noted that he missed an *o* in "Too."

In English, Landon had shared a poem he just started, titled: "People Who Should Shut Up About Cleaning Messes Considering Theirs Cost Us A Football Team." It fell ninety-nine words short of Ms. Edwards's suggested one hundred words. In fact, it was just one word: *Noah*.

"Look," Rina said, bending over to pick up a few newspapers that I missed, "you're just taking heat because of the football thing. Next issue we'll cover something stupid, like the dress code."

I pulled the papers from her hand and dumped them in the trash. "Whatever." I sort-of-by-accident pushed her aside with my shoulder on the way back to my locker.

"Noah." Rina made my name wobbly, like she was about to slip into a puddle.

I shoved my books into my backpack. "What?"

Rina grabbed the math textbook out of my locker and handed it to me. "You can't quit."

I shrugged. "Whatever."

That night, Ron called me. "Beating you to the punch, kid. That girlfriend of yours posted your essay all over the freakin' place. Got half of West Virginia breathing down my throat. We've got three guys—my whole crew—out searching for tracks. I'll let you know if we hear anything. Don't call me until tomorrow."

"Thanks, Ron," I mumbled.

There was a long pause on the other end. "You okay, kid?"

I just hung up.

"What's wrong with you?" Jeff asked in the morning. I guess we were talking again. He had gotten the mail and tossed another of Mom's letters onto the table. I ignored it.

"Nothing." I thumbed through the posts on Bucket Bear's Facebook page. I scrolled down to where Rina had added my column. Fifty comments. Some were from kids at school.

Noah Brickle needs to shut the hell up.

Bet Noah's mom was so proud, she toasted him all night. Oh, wait.

Let's not forget, we wouldn't even need this bucket challenge if it weren't for trash like Noah and his mom.

Even worse, though, were comments from parents.

From Mike's dad: *This kid needs a swift kick in the butt.*

From Brenna's mom: *Anyone else bothered that Noah Brickle gets a column in the school newspaper? Of all the kids in Ashtown?*

From Landon's mom: *This, coming from a kid who gave a mentally challenged boy a concussion on the football field. Worry less about doing right by bears, Noah, and more about making up for your own mistakes.*

I closed Facebook.

"You only had two bowls of cereal." Jeff shook the box. "You sick?"

I chewed my lip. "Maybe I should stay home today."

Jeff rocked back on his chair. "Sorry, kid. I've got a packed day. No playing hooky for either of us." He dumped more Frosted Flakes in my bowl. "Eat up."

I chomped on the flakes as Jeff coated them in milk. He cleared his throat. "I, um, read your article."

"Column," I corrected with a mouthful of mushy cereal. "Articles aren't opinion. Columns are."

"Right." Jeff stood, grabbing the milk and putting it in the fridge. He rubbed the top of my head as he passed me. "I'm proud of you."

I let my head slink down to the table. The tiger on

the box of cereal seemed to be pointing its finger at my forehead.

My cell phone vibrated, jolting me. The box wobbled and fell from the table. I scrambled for it, but the flakes scattered across the floor. The text from Rina was just a link to an Associated Press article. I clicked on it, and there was my mug again, this time next to the bear. "Boy Rallies to Save Bucket Bear" was the headline. The phone beeped again. *Dude! You're national news!*

Jeff leaned over my shoulder, reading the article. "Huh," he said. Flakes crunched under his feet as he dumped his coffee cup in the sink. "But you've still got to clean up this mess."

Sweeping up all the cereal made me late, and I missed the bus. Walking to school felt like moving through a cloud. It wasn't really raining; more like dampness hung all around us. The sweatshirt clung to my arms and moisture beaded on my hair. I wished I had an umbrella. For some reason, I thought of the dinosaur rain boots I outgrew when I was four. Man, I loved those. I wore them every day of the week, all summer long, even when Mom told me I couldn't bring them in the house anymore because they smelled like cheese. Now my toes squished in my soupy sneakers.

Maybe they'd shrink, and I'd finally get a new pair. I knew Jeff didn't have the money to buy things like clothes and shoes just because. The only new things I saw him buy were packs of cigarettes, and then he only got two packs a month. Just enough for one smoke to start and end the day. Plus, it's not like I was his kid. He told me to let him know if I ever needed anything, but what was I supposed to say? "Hey, you know these hundred-dollar sneakers Mom bought before she got drunk and ran that stop sign? The ones she bought a size too big so I'd grow into them? Well, they're too red and shiny. Sort of like that stop sign. How 'bout you buy me something black and cheap?"

The mist was so cold. Soon, there would be snow.

I was so lost in the cloud I trudged through I didn't even notice the squelching steps just behind me until Landon pushed against my shoulder as he passed me. "Hey!" I called, stumbling a little to the side.

He didn't turn around or slow his pace.

Suddenly I was the one pushing, my hands shoving him from behind. Not hard, just enough to make him lose his step. He whirled around, his arms up. "Back off, Sneaks!"

"What is your problem?" I didn't back off, but took a half step forward instead, so his nose was just a couple inches from mine. We were still the exact same size.

Landon tried to turn away from me, but I grabbed

his shoulder. He shrugged off my hand but faced me again. "Are you serious?"

I shoved my hands in my pockets and breathed through my nose. "I didn't do anything to you," I said quietly. "Look, I'm sorry we don't have the football team, but I didn't—"

This time Landon stepped toward me. I backed up at the sight of his boiling face. "How can you say you didn't do anything to me? You cost me everything. *Everything!*"

"You?" I yelled. "You? I lost my mom. I lost our team. I'm the loser here, not you."

"You got that much right," Landon spit. "You're a freaking loser. At that championship game, I asked you all night what was wrong. You didn't say a word. Then Micah's bleeding, and you're benched. Coach quits. Your mom . . . "

"When do we get the part where I did something to *you*?"

"I LOST THEM, TOO!"

"Who?" I shouted back. "Who did you lose?"

"You! Your family!" Landon's whole body shook. His head fell forward like it was on a hinge. And I remembered: Landon and I doing homework with Mom hovering behind us, a hand on each of our shoulders. Me, getting mad that Jeff threw the ball to Landon twice as much as me, and Jeff whispering that we'd get to play later, Landon only had then. Mom and Jeff's voices hoarse from cheering when Landon scored touchdown after touchdown, more than making up for the empty seat on the bench for Landon's mom. Landon chewing licorice and swapping stories with Glen at the Shop on Sundays. Landon running into the yard, whooping and waving a paper from the League, saying his football fee was waived thanks to a donation, and Jeff suddenly ducking inside the house.

And I remembered the times I had gone to Landon's house, where it was so cold we wore our coats inside. Where even with the lights on, the rooms seemed dim. No one in Ashtown was rolling in cash, but Landon had it extra hard. All their savings dried up after his dad died, and his mom worked second shift, three in the afternoon to eleven at night, at the canning factory. She would leave a note with instructions to pick up his brother from the neighbors and warm up some soup for dinner, to give the baby a bath, and go to bed by nine. I remember when I figured out that meant Landon didn't see his mom until the weekend, and not caring anymore that he leaned toward my mom like a sunflower to the light. I remembered the look in his eyes when Mom asked him to come to Jeff's house after school, so she could spend time with the baby.

I wondered if Landon could see these memories flying by behind my eyes like a movie on fast forward because he stared at me, still just inches from my face. "You shut me out," he said, much quieter. "I came to the Shop every day after school for a week. For a month."

I squeezed shut my eyes trying not to remember, but seeing Landon, his baby brother on his hip, standing in the lobby. Me, curling in a corner of the Shop, bricked in with shame. Glen telling him I didn't want to see anyone.

Landon pushed my shoulder again, but much softer. More like a, "Hey, listen to me!" than a real shove. His voice cold as ice, Landon said, "It didn't have to go that far. If you had just stood up. Not checked out. I would've gone with you to Coach. Did you know I went to the League? I asked them not to shut us down? If you had gone with me, explained things, maybe we would've had a chance. If you would've said sorry to Micah, maybe his mom would've backed off.

"You're a coward." Landon turned his back to me again. His bulky backpack knocked my chest. "You should've tried. You should've done something."

"I'm sorry," I whispered, but he already had disappeared in the fog.

Something he said floated back to me. I'm not sure what he said, but it sounded like, "I miss her, too."

CHAPTER FIFTEEN

Jeff had said this Bucket Bear attention would die down after a few days, but it had been almost two weeks and we still had newscasters calling the house to interview me and half the school still laughed as I walked by. "Bucket Boy" was a common chant. Very creative. The other half—Bruins players and cheerleaders mostly—hissed or threw stuff. Oh, and the environmental group invited me to join their ranks. That wouldn't have been so bad had they not been in the middle of a "natural cleansing" mission—which seemed to mean not washing at all. I didn't want to subject my nostrils to that.

Even now, Mike, Landon, and a couple other Bruins meatheads leaned against the lockers across the hall, laughing too loudly to be saying anything nice and staring too hard for whatever they were saying to be about anyone but me.

"What's with the white?" I asked Rina as she headed down the hall toward our lockers.

Rina looked like an angel sent from above after all

of that, and not just because she wore a long white dress. Rina was usually decked out in head-to-toe black. She seemed especially tall, gliding the wrong way in a tide of orange and black.

She shrugged. "I wasn't feeling too Bruins patriotic. Plus Micah's coming over tonight, so I felt like dressing up a little. He makes a big deal out of stuff like me wearing dresses." Rina's cheeks shined a little.

I was going to say that she looked pretty, but I thought she'd deck me. "How is Micah?" I asked instead, suddenly not able to look up from the stuck zipper on my backpack. I put the bag on the ground and yanked at it.

"He's fine." She opened her locker and grabbed a couple books to transfer into her backpack. "Great, actually. I know he'd like to see you."

My hand jerked so hard the zipper gave, and I fell back on my heels. "I doubt that."

"No, really," Rina said. "Micah . . . he's not like the rest of us. Like, once we had this god-awful family reunion where Grandpa forgot his teeth, Uncle Harry popped the head off my little sister's Barbie and made her cry, and my great-aunt Sally's deviled eggs went bad and made everyone puke. Micah was sickest of us all. You know what he remembers about it?" Rina smiled. "That his hospital cot had wheels like a train." She closed her locker. "He only remembers the good. All he talks about is how much fun he had with you and the rest of the guys last year."

I piled my books on the ground outside my locker, sorting which to shove inside and which to take home. "I don't know, Rina. The rest of us—your mom, for example—aren't like that."

Rina sighed, putting my math book back in my bag. "You're going to need this. Quiz Monday, remember?" She waited until I looked up before continuing. "You could tell him you're sorry. If you saw him, that is. Might be nice. You know, move on." She held up her fairy tale book. "'And they all lived happier ever after.'"

"Shouldn't it be 'happily ever after'?"

"Just being realistic."

I shook my head. "You might be the smartest person I know," I said as Rina's mouth twitched, "but you're pretty dumb sometimes. It's a little late for happily ever after. Or happier." I popped open my locker.

"Watch out!" Rina shouted.

But it was too late. A full bucket of orange energy drink tipped as I opened my locker door, straight down my head and soaking my body. The bucket, a metal gardening type, slammed into my head and hit the ground with a familiar-sounding clatter.

"Calm down," said Rina, even though I hadn't moved or spoken. She yanked a sweatshirt from the mountain of junk in her locker and patted my head with a sleeve. "Don't go all *Carrie* on us."

I stood in a puddle of orange, my hair dripping into my eyes, not moving, not speaking.

"The *Carrie* thing was a joke! Did—did they actually fill the bucket with blood, too?" gasped Rina, just as I realized what was streaming down my face was too warm and thick to be energy drink. *It's blood.* The thought seemed separate than me, even as the red dripped down my forehead. *It's* my *blood.*

"Oh, geez! Oh, crap!" Rina gasped. She pressed the sweatshirt against my head and turned toward the crowd gathered behind us. Funny, I hadn't heard them, hadn't heard anyone but Rina, until that moment.

Now they roared like a waterfall—laughing, hooting, chanting, "Bring back the Bruins!"—while I stood like a statue. Just as quick, I felt pain across the top of my head where the bucket hit, like someone held a flaming lighter against the skin.

"Somebody get help!" Rina screamed. I wobbled a little, sort of falling forward against the lockers. Rina wedged herself between me and the lockers, holding me upright and cradling my head with both hands. "Come on! Someone help him!" Slowly the buzz of the crowd simmered to a hiss.

Someone help him! I clenched shut my eyelids, but couldn't block out another image. Micah, pale and whimpering, sprawled on his back in the grass. I tried to back up, but Rina wouldn't let me go.

"It's just Gatorade," I heard Landon say as I sank to my knees. He was next to Rina, his face twisted. I slumped forward into him and Rina. The last thing I remember is the rush of feet as teachers ran toward me.

Just a concussion. *Just.*

That's just what happened to Micah.

What was it with lying on a hospital cot that made me relive the worst memories? Because now, in the hospital, I closed my eyes and finally fully relived the championship game.

That day, I had been keeping my mouth shut about what had happened to Mom the night before.

Only Jeff knew, and he sat alone on the bleachers, not even looking at the game at all. Mom, who had been released from the state police barracks that morning, stayed curled in a ball in Jeff's bedroom. I was hollow inside, nothing more than the helmet and pads and jersey. Landon kept asking what was up, why wasn't I buzzing like everyone else. "This is the championships!" My best friend grabbed my shoulders and shook until my face made something like a smile.

I looked to the bleachers and saw the empty spot

next to Jeff, where Mom was supposed to be. How could she do this to me?

Her face, a cartoon picture of shock with a circle mouth and backdrop of blue lights, flashed behind my closed eyes. *Don't tell them, Noah!*

When she went to jail, what would happen to me? She was so selfish. So stupid. So weak. I tuned into Coach Abram's orders, but I couldn't shake the fury filling me.

I heard Coach Abrams giving Micah the okay to head out. We were so far ahead, it didn't matter if the ball slipped through Micah's slow-moving hands like it was greased. We'd still win. Micah needed Coach's help getting his helmet on. His grin was so wide as he trotted out to the field that his mouthpiece kept falling out. He wasn't nervous. Micah never worried about anything at all.

We were on the ten-yard line, poised for another touchdown. The crowd surged with applause as Micah turned and waved to them. *Like a favorite pet doing a special trick.* My thoughts were cruel. "Simple pitch play," Coach shouted my way.

Focus! I took the snap and mimed handing the ball to Landon as he rammed his way down the line of scrimmage. Meanwhile, I tossed the ball to Micah, who was hovering just along the outside. He was supposed to cut down Landon's pass. It's the only move he ever had to make. All he had to do is follow the plan. All he had to do is this one job. That's it!

Mom's job was to take care of me. ("Don't tell them I was drinking, Noah!")

But Micah just stood there, gaping around, doing nothing.

I should've stopped her. I should've been paying attention to her glassy eyes. I should've noticed her wine-stained lips. I should've heard the twang in her voice. I could've stopped her.

"Go!" I screamed to Micah. "Move! Do something!" But he stared around at the crowd, the ball barely held in limp fingers.

And I wasn't planning on it. I wasn't meaning to do it.

Yet, I was moving. I rushed him, about to rip the ball from his hands. My shoulder hit him from the front. The defensive tackle rammed him from behind. *Crunch!* Sweat flew from Micah onto my face. He pulled back on the ball and I yanked it free, slamming him again. *Crunch!* His cry was like a squeak. Micah's helmet slammed against my shoulder gear. But I didn't stop, I ran, knocking over everyone in my path. Stepping on them, over them. I was in the end zone—the quarterback—scoring the touchdown just as the buzzer rings.

No one cheered. No one moved. Because there was Micah, sprawled where I slammed into him. Not getting

up. Not moving at all. Coach rushed toward him, shout-
ing for an ambulance. Landon's face twisted, looking at
me like he didn't know me. Like I was a monster. Jeff
put his head in his hands. Micah's mom sobbed on the
field beside him.

And me, I stood alone.

I sat up on the edge of the hospital cot, waiting for
Jeff to get there so we could go home. The nurses were
too nice, pushing my hair back to look at my head,
asking me if they could bring me a blanket or the
remote for the television in the little curtained-off
room I shared with an old man. Not sure why the
old guy was in the emergency room, except that every
now and then he'd moan and fart, making the room
smell worse than the time the school cafeteria served
roasted cauliflower.

The curtain flew back with a *whoosh,* and Jeff
rushed into me like a linebacker. He didn't pause, just
flew into the room and crushed me against him. He
smelled like motor oil and the cinnamon he shakes into
his coffee. "Jesus, Noah. What the hell happened?"

I shrugged, face still burrowed into his shoulder.
For a second my chin wobbled. If he weren't holding
me together I'd swear I was made of cobwebs, ready to
fly apart. I swallowed and pushed back a little. Jeff held

onto my shoulders, looking in my eyes. His forehead creased into deep lines.

"What?" I asked when he didn't stop staring.

Jeff shrugged. "Good thing Halloween's coming up. You'd be a great Frankenstein."

My hands flew up to the bandage on my head, a few inches above my hairline. "The doc said the stitches were small, that's why they needed six of them. How bad is it?"

Jeff smiled, but it looked more like a wince. "Just busting you, kid. That mop of hair will cover them, anyway." Just as quick the smile melted away. "What am I going to tell Diane?"

I stared at my hands. "Don't tell her anything. The stitches will be out before she is."

"Noah," Jeff said softly. He sat beside me on the cot, making the paper cover crinkle. "I'm going to have to tell her."

I shrugged.

He draped his arm around my shoulder, then let it fall to his side. "Just got to fill out some paperwork and then you're free to go." Jeff's nose crinkled as he stood. "It smells like Sunny D mixed with exhaust in here."

After Jeff left, I lay back on the cot and closed my eyes. I almost fell asleep, too, but the squeak of steps and the soft rustle of the curtain woke me. My eyes fluttered open and there was Landon, holding the curtain back with fingertips, half in and half out of the room. I got the feeling that if I hadn't opened my eyes just then, he would've left. Even now, Landon looked like he was caught cheating on a test.

"It smells like crap in here," he said when our eyes met.

From the other side of the curtain, the old man said, "Sorry." Then he moaned and farted again.

Landon's mouth twitched and I lost it, covering my laugh with the inside of my elbow. Landon let the curtain fall behind him, coughing to hide his own laughter. It didn't work. Soon we were both doubled over, choking on silent bellows. Then the old man shifted with a crinkle of his own paper-covered cot and another toxic cloud drifted toward us with a moan. No chance of hiding our laughter that time.

"Want a seat?" I asked, throwing out my elbow toward the space beside me on the cot.

Landon shook his head. "I don't want to stay. I just needed to make sure . . . I didn't mean . . . "

I nodded. "Couldn't find a plastic bucket, huh?"

Landon stared at his sneakers. "It was my idea, but our bucket is missing. Mike brought his, set it all up. I didn't know he'd bring a gardening bucket like that. A metal one." His Adam's apple bobbed as he swallowed. I noticed the rust-colored stains on the shoulder of his orange Bruin's sweatshirt and realized it was blood. My blood. Landon slowly looked up. "I should've stopped him." Landon didn't say anything for a few seconds. Then, "What now?"

"I don't know."

Landon nodded. "Me, either. You going to tell Mr. Anderson?"

"Nah," I said, not looking at him. He came here to make sure he wasn't going to get in trouble. That was it. The thought was an animal clawing its way out of my belly. Stupid. Stupid to think he was there to make sure I was okay, when it was really just to ensure he was all right.

"So you're not going to catch any heat, okay? You can go now." I lay back down on the cot with a flop and squeezed shut my eyes.

When I peeked back, Landon was pulling back the curtain, his back to me. But he wasn't leaving. "I'm sorry."

"It's just a couple stitches."

Landon shook his head. "Not just that. I'm sorry. For what happened to you."

I turned away from him.

"Mom's on first shift instead of second tomorrow," he said.

"Congratulations."

"I was gonna . . . " Landon sighed.

"Spit it out, already. I'm supposed to be resting."

"I was gonna look for some tracks. Bear tracks. Dad taught me how."

I rolled onto my back. Landon never, ever talked about his dad. I pushed up so I was seated, facing him. He was breathing hard, shoulders going up and down, like he was the patient, the one in pain. "He liked to hunt. My dad, I mean."

I nodded, not wanting to break the spell of Landon talking to me, talking about his dad.

Landon twisted his neck. "So if you want to look for tracks, let me know."

Just then, Jeff pushed the curtain back further. "Hey, Landon," he said, like the fact that my former best friend was here was totally not a surprise. Narrowing his eyes at me, Jeff added, "Noah's going to be tied up tomorrow until late afternoon. We're visiting his mom."

"No, I'm not." I crossed my arms.

"Look, kid, she's going to bust out of there if she doesn't see for herself that you're okay tomorrow. You're doing it."

"No."

Landon cleared his throat. "I've got to watch Henry until three o'clock, anyway. We can head out then."

"Great," Jeff said. "I'm not sure if bear hunting is following the doctor's orders to lay low, though."

"We're not hunting, just tracking," I said.

"And if you find this bear? What are you going to do then?"

"Call the authorities," Landon and I said at the same time. Landon's smile looked like a fishhook pulled back the side of his mouth, and I knew both of us were thinking the same thing—if we spotted the bear, we'd save her. Ourselves. "See you tomorrow," he said.

CHAPTER SIXTEEN

We didn't talk on the drive home from the hospital. Jeff turned into the pharmacy and didn't say anything then, either. Just slammed his door shut and took quick steps to the store. I stayed in the truck. A few minutes later, he tossed the shopping bag onto my lap. Inside was a combination lock for my locker, a bottle of ginger ale, and a pack of vanilla cookies.

Again, I forgot that I wasn't talking to Jeff and held up the cookies. "What are these for?"

Jeff's shoulder popped up and down. "My dad used to get those and ginger ale for me whenever I was sick."

"But I'm not sick." I fingered the bandage on my head, trying to picture Jeff as a kid. I couldn't do it.

Jeff shrugged again.

When we got home, he actually darted around the truck to open my door for me. "It's cool, Jeff. I can walk."

"Shut up. The doc said you might be wobbly." He hovered just beside me up the walkway to the house. "Sit down," he ordered, pointing to the couch.

Funny, we almost never used the living room. The big, plaid couch was older than me. The boxy television was almost as ancient. It always seemed like Jeff and I hung out in the kitchen, watching the TV in there while we ate dinner. But I sank into the couch and Jeff handed me the remote. When he just stayed there, staring at me, I tore open the cookies and crammed one in my mouth. "Don't you have to get the Shop?"

Jeff crossed his arms. "Glen's running things today." He continued just standing there.

"Want one?" I held up another cookie.

Jeff grabbed the cookie and sank into the other end of the couch. I flipped on the television, and just stuck with the Discovery Channel's Bigfoot documentary, even though we had seen it a couple weeks ago. My eyes had just drifted shut when Jeff tucked a blanket around me. Softly he said, "You worried me, kid."

I'm not sure how long I was out, but when the doorbell rang, the room's only light came from the television, where a show about the formation of the galaxy now played. I tried to sit up, but my head pounded. Jeff popped up and flipped on the porch light. "I've got it, Noah," he said. "Keep resting."

Jeff opened the door and there was Ms. Jacobs,

standing there in her high heels. She winked at Jeff. "Hey, handsome neighbor."

"Sorry, Cathy," said Jeff, already half shutting the door. "If those raccoons are back, I can't help right now."

"Oh, Jeff," said Ms. Jacobs, her voice sugary. "I heard what happened to that boy today. You've had your hands full, haven't you?" She stepped forward and put a hand on Jeff's chest as she spoke. He took a step backward, but she just moved forward, like he had invited her in instead of moving away from her.

I rolled onto my side on the couch, burying my face in the nubby plaid.

"Noah's doing fine, thanks. Now's not a good time, though. He's resting." I heard the creak of the door and figured Jeff was trying to scoot her out.

"Oh, but I've brought you—you and Noah—something. I figured it's been a while since you've had something homemade." The smell of hamburger and potatoes wafted into the room. My stomach grumbled. Traitor stomach. "Just thought you could use a woman's touch." Ms. Jacobs's voice turned to honey.

Jeff coughed. "Thanks, Cath. Appreciate it. But the kid and I are doing fine." His voice hardened. "You shouldn't have gone to the trouble."

"Oh, no trouble at all!" Ms. Jacobs replied. "After all you've done for that kid. Takes a village, you know."

Jeff didn't say anything.

"Do you have a couple plates?" The door creaked again, and I heard Ms. Jacobs's heels click on the foyer tile. "Some napkins? Best to eat it while it's hot. Maybe you and I could just have a nibble while Noah sleeps."

"Not now, Cathy," Jeff said, even as I heard those heels click across into the kitchen.

"Nonsense! No trouble at all!"

A cabinet door opened and closed and plates clattered onto the table. "See?" Ms. Jacobs singsonged. "Still remember my way around here, even after all this time. You remember how we used to have dinner together. Dessert, too. Remember?"

The doorway between the kitchen and living room croaked as Jeff leaned against it, halfway in the living room with me and half in the kitchen. "It's been a long time, Cathy," Jeff said. If Ms. Jacobs's voice were honey, his was bark, rough and crumbly. "Thanks for the dinner, but I'm not hungry. I'll eat with my kid."

"But he's not *your kid*, is he?" Ms. Jacobs said, the sweetness gone. "How long has been since Diane left?"

Another croak of floorboards. Cabinet door opening. Plates clattering back on their stack inside. "She comes home in a week."

"Then what?"

"Then what *what*, Cathy?"

"Well, you've stepped up. Done your part. You have nothing to feel guilty about, Jeff." The click of her heels moved closer to the doorway. Toward Jeff. "You've done more than enough. Once she's out, she can take the boy and move on, too."

"Now's not a good—" The trill of the phone broke off Jeff's words. He picked it up. "Diane! It's Friday, I wasn't expecting to hear from—"

Voice too high, Ms. Jacobs laughed. "Where do you keep the corkscrew, Jeffy? I'll pop open a bottle of wine for us to have with dinner!"

"No, no, Diane. Cathy's just leaving. That's not— no!" I peeked over the couch arm. Jeff covered the receiver with his palm. "You need to leave, Cathy. Just grab your casserole, and get out."

"There's no need to be so rude!" She stomped toward the door.

"Your meatloaf!" Jeff pointed to the table.

"Keep it! Choke on it!" Cathy slammed shut the door.

Quickly, I lay back down. Too quickly, because I knocked my head on the arm and gasped at how it throbbed. I squeezed shut my eyes, feeling Jeff staring at the top of my head.

He sighed. "It's not what it sounded like, Diane." Long pause. "He's fine. He's sleeping. Want me to wake up him? . . . Yes, I know. I know. Look, the doc gave me all these instructions. I don't know . . . Yep. Talked to the principal."

Jeff's voice turned cold. "I'm handling it, okay? Yes. Yes! I've got the kid painkillers. The doc said to let him sleep. I'm taking care of it, all right?" he boomed. "Just like I have been for the past six months. I'm. Handling. It."

Jeff sighed and put his hand—phone still in it—at his side. "Look, I just . . . I'm in over my head with this kid. I need you back here. I'm not cut out . . . "

I strained to hear as Jeff moved to the back porch, but the doorbell rang again.

Storming into the kitchen, I grabbed the huge casserole dish of meatloaf and whipped open the door, ready to throw it in Ms. Jacobs's face. Instead, Rina stood in front of me, Micah in her shadow.

Rina's eyes fluttered from the bandage on my head to the meatloaf in my arms and back up to my eyes. "Got any plates? A fork, maybe? Or are you going to T-Rex that meatloaf right out of the dish?"

I put a chunk of meatloaf onto four plates and brought them to the table, leaving a spot empty for Jeff even though Mom's fifteen minutes were up and he still hadn't come back inside. For a long time, none of us said anything, just shoveled the meatloaf into our mouths. Ms. Jacobs might be a man-stealing jerk, but she makes a mean meatloaf.

"Hmm, this is awesome," Rina said. She rubbed

her belly and leaned back in the chair. "Mom's making roasted beets and chickpeas for dinner. Thank God we stopped by when we did."

"Chickpeas look like tiny butts," I blurted when no one said anything for a minute. Micah just sat there, smiling at me.

Rina cocked an eyebrow. "How bad was that concussion?"

"I thought we were just going for a walk, Rina," said Micah, his mouth crammed with potato. "I like this walk."

Rina smiled at her cousin and touched his big hand with her fingertips. "We don't need to tell Aunt Sarah we stopped by Noah's house, okay?"

Micah nodded, smiling. "I like Noah. I miss Noah." To me, he said, "We play football. Right, Noah?"

My breath didn't seem to bring enough air to my lungs and my head ached. I don't think it had anything to do with my concussion. How could he sit there, smiling at me like this? He should hate me. Rina should hate me. I rubbed at the bandage. "We don't play football anymore."

"Did you get hurt, too?" Micah pointed at my head.

"Yeah, Micah, he did get hurt," Rina answered when I couldn't.

"You'll get better, Noah." He scooped up another bite. "I did. I'm better."

I nodded, my throat choked with too many words for any to come out.

"Yes, you did," Rina told Micah, but her eyes stayed on me. "You got better, didn't you? Almost right away."

"Yeah." Micah sighed. "But Mom says no more football for me. I miss playing."

"I have a football outside," I heard myself say. "We could play a little now. If you want."

If Jeff was surprised to see Rina and Micah as we came out on the back porch he didn't say anything. "Take it easy," was all he murmured when I rooted out the football from under all the leaves in the yard. He stubbed out his cigarette and rubbed at his face with his hands. Rina sat in the grass in front of him. The two of them had the same expression, eyes wide and happy, mouths hard and worried. "If that ball hits you in the head, Diane will kill me," Jeff called.

Micah, though, he was pure joy as he trotted across the yard. He squatted, both hands out. "Throw it here, Noah! I'm ready!"

I tossed the ball so gently it fell with a thud in the grass in front of Micah. "Come on!" he said and threw it back at me. "I'm ready!"

This time I threw it with just a little more force. It landed in Micah's hands. He whooped and ran around the yard like it was baseball instead of football. Jeff and Rina cheered him on, especially when he spiked the ball after a full circle. "Awesome, Micah!" I clapped as his face split with a grin.

Fifteen minutes and just as many homerun touch-downs later, Rina said she had to get back before her mom sent out a search party. "Or worse, burns the beets." Her nose wrinkled. "Ever smell burnt beets?"

"Thanks for stopping by," said Jeff as we walked them to the gate.

"No problem," Rina said.

Micah tossed the football hand to hand, still smiling. He handed it to me, but I handed it back. "You can have it."

"Really, Noah?"

I nodded. "I don't play anymore."

"Because you got hurt?"

I tried to say no but my throat closed again. Micah pressed the ball into my arms. "You'll get better," he said. "Just like me."

"I'm sorry," I whispered, the words snagging like briars on the way out. "I'm so sorry, Micah."

I didn't think he'd know what I meant. After all, he had been so happy to see me. To play football with me. That had to mean he didn't remember, right? Mom once told me that Micah "has some missing connections." So I figured he didn't remember I was the one who had hurt him. But Micah pushed the ball toward me with more force. I looked into his face. "I forgive you," he said. He let go of the ball and I held onto it.

For just a second the smile he always wore was gone. Just as quick it came back. "You'll get better. I did." He pointed to the football. "We can play again."

I guess I stumbled a little because suddenly Jeff was there, arm around me, holding me up.

"Hang on a sec!" Rina called out to Micah as the gate clicked shut. She darted back in front of us. Jeff squeezed my shoulder and stepped back as Rina leaned in and whispered, "Want to take it back?"

"Take what back?"

She crossed her arms, the moonlight making her smile shine and her eyes glitter. Her breath frosted the air in little white clouds. "I seem to remember you saying something about it being too late? About me being pretty dumb? You know, right before that bucket slammed into your skull."

Jeff snorted and walked back toward the house. He whistled under his breath.

"You were right," I muttered.

"And are you . . . Oh, I don't know . . . *happier* right now?"

"Yes, Rina." I laughed.

From down the street, a voice called, "*Rina! Micah! Dinner's ready!*"

"That's my mom," said Rina, turning toward the

sound. Without thinking, I leaned in, pressing my lips against the soft curve of her cheek. Slowly Rina tilted her head back, our faces brushing. I caught a whiff of her spearmint hair.

I know I should've said something—anything—as we stood too closely there in the moonlight, Micah just behind us and her mom calling her away. But all I could do is smile. Rina bounced a little on her toes and then trotted away, her hand pressed against her cheek.

When I got back into the house, Jeff sat at the table, ankle crossed over his knee, empty plate of meatloaf on his lap, and a wicked smile across his face.

I turned my back to him. I went to the sink and filled it with water and squirts of dish soap. Still not looking at him, even when he chuckled, I scrubbed at our dirty plates and forks. "What?"

"Must've been some knock in the head, that's all."

"Why does everyone keep saying that?"

Jeff laughed again as he slipped his plate into the basin of water and picked up the towel to dry.

CHAPTER SEVENTEEN

I'm not getting up," I told Jeff when he woke me in the morning.

"I'm not getting in the car," I said when he told me it was time to leave.

"I'm not going in," I promised when he parked in the visitors' lot at the Center Regional Jail.

"You have to go in," Jeff said. "I can't leave you here." He pointed to a sign in the parking lot. "No unaccompanied minors may be left in vehicles."

"So we go home." I fastened my seat belt.

Jeff unsnapped the buckle. "It's Saturday, the only day in the week that Diane can have visitors." He faced the wheel again and for just a second, his always-calm-always-cool manner melted and he was . . . I don't know the word for it. *Raw* comes close. He was raw and jagged like a just-popped blister from a burn. The kind that aches when even air touches it. Jeff slammed the heels of his hands against the wheel.

"For more than six months, she's asked if you were coming to visit. When I said no, for six months she just dealt with it. But now? She's insisting I bring you. She's counting on it. And, damn it, Noah!" Slowly the cool, calm mask rebuilt across his face. When he continued, it was with the unwavering, steady voice he always used. "Noah, man up. Go in there and see her. She needs this. *I* need this. You need this, more than any of us."

Scooting as far from him as I could, I pressed my forehead against the cool glass of the window. The sky around us was a blanket of gray, leaves ripped from trees in the blustery wind peppering the air. Winter was coming. "I don't want to see her."

I closed my eyes, letting the never-ending film of my life with Mom play in full color behind the lids. The scenes were mushed and out of order, memories from years before flipping seamlessly into much more recent ones. I saw her arms open wide as I stepped off the bus from kindergarten. Heard her laugh when Jeff and I said something at the same time. Felt her hand covering my much smaller one as I crunched leaves under my dino rain boots. Breathed in her lavender-scented hair when she kissed the top of my head as I did homework at the kitchen table. "I love you," echoed again and again in my skull. That's how every moment with her began or ended. "I love you."

I rapped my head against the window glass, trying to halt the scenes about to come. I didn't want to hear her say she loved me in jail. I didn't want this. I didn't want to be here. I didn't want to see her there. It was stupid. I knew it was stupid. I was being like Landon's baby brother, pitching a fit because the day was over. Stupid. Stupid. Stupid. *Rap, rap, rap.*

My eyes still were shut when Jeff opened my car door, just as I was about to bang my head against the window again. "Not even another concussion is going to stop us from going in there," he warned. Jeff's fingers parted my hair to check the Band-Aid. Funny how such a little cut had caused so much blood. Today the cut just looked like a slug with black stitches threaded through it.

"Is it okay?" I asked.

"Yep." He smoothed my hair over it. "She would've freaked if you knocked it open."

"I don't want to do this," I said again.

Jeff laughed, but it was bitter. Mean. "What makes you think I do? You think I want this? Any of this?" His hand swept over the parking lot, the jail, me. "It'll be over soon," he added. "One more week 'til she's out, Noah. Then it—all of this—will be over."

All of this over. No more fill-in parenting for Jeff. No more kid to deal with. No more taking care of me just because he felt guilty for leaving that night.

I followed Jeff into the visitors' entrance, trying not to see the other families making their way in, but not able to block them out, either. A little girl skipped past us. A lady who smelled like fast food pushed into me as I reached for the door. A dozen or so people who looked like they could be going anywhere, on the way to the grocery store or heading to the park. Not like their heart was ping-ponging in an empty body, all their insides having turned to slosh. Inside, my eyes swept the room. I slunk into a chair next to the only other person who looked as freaked out as me—a man in a business suit and gray hair. He held a picture of a little girl in his hands, fingering the corners of the photograph so much they curled in.

I slouched in the seat. When I sat upright, my legs shook. The doors opened again, bringing with it a blast of cold air. I zipped my coat and ducked into it.

"Noah," Jeff called from his spot in front of a big window. On the other side of the glass, a bored-looking woman in an officer's uniform stared at me with dull eyes. She beckoned me with curled fingers.

As I got up to go toward them, my phone dinged with a text. I pulled it out of my pocket. It was from Ron, the DNR officer. *Bucket Bear spotted in woods behind your house. Tracking now. Keep you updated.*

"We have to go!" I called to Jeff. "The bear! They're tracking her! She's at our house!"

"What?" Jeff shook his head and held up a hand. "Later. Now we're visiting your mom."

"But—" I didn't bother finishing. Jeff's face turned to stone.

"He's going to have remove his coat." The guard pointed to a row of lockers. "Are you chewing gum?" she asked me.

I nodded, and she pointed to the trash can. "No gum allowed."

I stared at her, trying to see if it was a joke. I mean, seriously? What could a prisoner do with gum that was so awful? When I didn't move, Jeff tilted his head toward the trash can. I sighed and stomped over to it, spitting the oh-so-dangerous Bubble Yum inside. Whatever.

"There are vending machines in the visiting room," Jeff muttered. "I'll get you more gum."

"Don't bother."

The guard pointed to the lockers, so I headed over there. "Got anything in your pockets, put it in there," she said. After I stuffed my jacket inside went back to Jeff, she continued. "These are the rules—"

"Becky, you see me every week. Do you really have to go through all this? I'll keep the kid in line," Jeff said.

Prison Guard Becky didn't even glance at him. "Jeff," I interrupted. "We've got to make this quick. They spotted the bear. I want to be there when they find her!"

Jeff's mouth twisted and that mask slipped just an inch. "*This* is where you are, Noah. Pay attention."

"May I continue?" Becky snapped. When neither of us spoke, she went on. "No gum, no jackets."

"I know," I grunted.

Becky didn't react, just kept spouting off rules. "No unaccompanied minors. No personal belongings outside of the locker. You go through the metal detector and make way to your table. You hug hello but no lengthy embracing and no touching after that. No loud exchanges. No sudden movements. No outbursts of any sort. Visits end at the guards' discretion."

"We got it, Becky," Jeff said.

She punched a few buttons on her computer keyboard. "She's got someone with her now. I'm going to check with the guard about whether she can have three visitors at a time."

"Who's visiting her?" asked Jeff, surprise in his voice.

But Becky leveled him with her glare. "Have a seat."

Jeff had warned me that it might be a couple of hours waiting before we'd get to see Mom. But the wait was too fast for me—a different officer called our names a few minutes later. I wanted to talk to Jeff about the bear. I even thought I'd heard my phone beeping new texts from the locker, but he wouldn't let me check it. Now Jeff smiled at me and held out his hand like I was a baby. I ignored the way my legs shook and shoved my hands in my pockets as we made our way toward the bulky officer. He didn't smile as we approached. If anything, his narrow eyes turned to slits. "What's in your hair?" he barked at me.

"Oh, the kid's got a Band-Aid," Jeff said casually, but his eyes were hard.

"Hold down your hair," the officer ordered. "Let me see it."

I did what he said, even though my arms wobbled like chicken wings. The officer wore gloves like a doctor. He pulled the edge of the Band-Aid back to see the cut underneath. The tug pulled on my hair, making my eyes sting. *Don't cry*, I ordered my stupid eyes. *Don't you dare cry.* The officer put back the bandage. His eyes met mine for a second, and he smiled, quick as a blink. I got the feeling he smiled a lot more when he wasn't wearing the uniform.

"Turn out your pockets," he ordered next. I followed Jeff's lead, and yanked out my pockets so they hung from my pants. The officer nodded and I tucked them back in. He turned and walked us through heavy metal doors.

Through another set of doors, I spotted a big room, like a cafeteria. Through the closed doors, I heard voices. Some argued. Someone else laughed. A baby cried. The officer opened one of the doors and the noise slammed against me. I stepped backward.

"I can't do this," I blurted, my knees turning to liquid.

"Come on, Noah," Jeff said. "Your mom's waiting for us in there."

"Are you coming in or not?" The officer let the door shut again with a snap when I leaned against the wall and closed my eyes. I was shaking so hard now I wasn't sure I could stand.

"Noah, enough of this crap!" Jeff's voice sharpened to an edge I had never heard before.

"Back off!" I yelled back. "Just leave me alone. Pretend it's a week from now."

"What's that supposed to mean?"

"I know you're just doing this—that you're just here—out of guilt. I know you're counting down until you're not stuck with me anymore!" I screamed all of it without opening my eyes. When I did, I saw Jeff just in front of the doors, his eyes wide and mouth hanging open like he was coated in concrete.

The officer cleared his throat. "Are you going in or what?"

"Noah," Jeff said after a long pause. He still didn't move. "How could you—"

The door opened again. Mom's sponsor, Trenton, stepped out. I guess that answered who had been visiting Mom before us. "What's going on?"

This time Trenton wore flannel and boots instead of a saggy suit. Next to him, the corrections officer stood with his arms crossed. "We either go in or we leave," he barked.

"Oh, come on, Stan," Trenton said. "Give the kid a break. Hasn't seen his mom in half a year."

"Not my monkeys, not my circus," the officer replied.

"Look, Noah," said Jeff, putting his hand on my shoulder. "Why don't you just go back to the lobby? Think about it a little more. I'll tell Diane you need a minute. Just don't take long. We only get two hours with her."

"Not a chance," Officer Stan barked. "No unaccompanied minors."

I watched Jeff's mask blister again. Trenton must've seen it, too, because he put a hand on Jeff's chest to cut off whatever he was going to say next. "I'll stay with the kid," he said. "You go in, see Diane. She's jumping out of her skin in there, worried about Noah. Great idea, by the way, telling her about the concussion."

"I couldn't help it," Jeff said. "I needed his medical history at the hospital."

Their words sounded so far away, like they were traveled down a tunnel toward me. *Maybe it's the concussion*, I lied to myself. But I knew the truth. I was blocking them out because I couldn't halt the thoughts ramming around my stupid skull. What would she look like? Would she be in black-and-white-striped pajama-looking clothes? Would she cry? Oh, God. I couldn't handle it if she cried. Would she cheer when she saw me? And—now my stomach bubbled like lava—how would I tell her goodbye? Because I would be leaving here and she wouldn't, not yet. I opened my eyes and there was Jeff. Another jolt of worry rushed through me. When she did come home, would he leave? I shook my head harder. "I can't do this."

CHAPTER EIGHTEEN

Trenton grabbed my elbow. "Go on, Jeff," he said. "We'll be there in a minute."

We went back to the lobby. I moved to sit in one of the empty chairs, but Trenton headed through the automatic doors so I followed him. I hadn't realized I was sweating until the cold air slammed against my cheeks. "Looked like you needed a change of scenery, Noah," he said.

I nodded, swallowing the cold air like a can of pop, letting it fill my lungs. Trenton leaned against the cement wall of the building. My legs stopped trying to pretend they weren't made of soup as I slumped down onto the ground. The cold walkway chilled my skin.

"Jeff ever tell you how far back we go?" Trenton asked a few minutes later. Truthfully, I had sort of forgotten he was there.

I shook my head. "You said you played ball in high school."

"That's right." Trenton's voice reminded me of how

I imagine a hound would talk. Every few words, it dipped into a sort of growl. "You remind me of him."

"Of who?"

"Of your dad."

"Jeff isn't my dad," I corrected.

Trenton laughed, but it, too, sounded like a growl. He sank down onto the cement beside me, even though the cement had to freeze the seat of his thin suit. "I always knew he was cut out for it, even though he said it'd never happen."

"Cut out for what?" Seriously, couldn't this guy see I was in the middle of a major freak-out?

"For being a dad."

"He's not my dad," I snapped again.

"He's your dad in any way that counts."

"Whatever. He's going to leave the minute Mom gets out of here."

Trenton barked out another bitter laugh. "Jeff's not going anywhere. Don't you know him by now? Look up loyalty on Google and his picture will show up." Trenton folded his hands behind his head. "I grew up the next block over from Jeff. He moved in with his dad when he was twelve."

This time, Trenton's laugh was smooth. "Most messed up kid you could imagine. Maybe that's what reminds me of you. Ah, don't look at me like that, kid.

You know you're messed up. I've got an eye for such things."

I gritted my teeth, too curious about Jeff to give in to how much I hated this guy. "What do you mean, he moved in with his dad? Where was he before?"

Trenton smirked, like he knew I was hooked. "Jeff never told you? He was a foster kid. Lived in something like twenty houses before moving in with ol' Mr. Convey."

I sucked on my bottom lip, thinking about it. Jeff never mentioned any family aside from his dad, never questioned why Mom and I didn't have anyone but each other. Made sense that it was because he didn't have anyone else, either.

Trenton continued, "Always a new kid at Convey's. Children's services would send him their worst cases, the ones everyone else gave up on. The kids would be with him, helping at the Shop until he'd whip them into shape, and then they'd get shipped back to their parents or wherever."

I rubbed my temples, trying to understand what Trenton was saying. "Where were Jeff's real parents?"

Trenton sighed. He pulled a Dum Dums lollipop from his pocket and unwrapped. "Want one?" he offered. I shook my head. "Well," he said, "he never knew his dad."

"Me, either," I blurted.

Trenton cocked an eyebrow in a "told-you" sort of way. "His mom was young. Only a teen when she had him. Never wanted the job, if you know what I mean. He . . . " Trenton sucked on the lollipop. "He should be the one to tell you this, about what happened next."

Trenton crunched the lollipop between his teeth and slowly stood up. "Come on, Noah." He held out his hand. When I didn't take it, he added, "You don't have to go in. Just back to that hallway we were in before, okay? I'll get your dad—Jeff—to come out to you. It's his story, not mine."

I let Trenton pull me to my feet. "You know," he said, "if you ever want to tell *your* story, that teen group still meets on Tuesdays."

"I'm fine."

Trenton's eyes raked over me. "Sure you are, kid."

The guard at the door sighed when Trenton asked to be let back in. He even went through the search all over again for me, even checking the bandage. Finally, he let us through.

Before I knew it, Jeff was in front of me.

"You didn't have a dad," I blurted. It wasn't a question.

Jeff nodded, his hands shoved in his pockets. Neither of us acknowledged the guard standing just beside us. "Not for a long time."

"Why didn't you ever tell me? Trenton said you were a foster kid."

Jeff pulled in a deep breath. "Not exactly my favorite topic of conversation."

When I didn't say anything for a moment, Jeff filled the silence. "I spent a lot of time with grandparents, then they checked out, too. Think I was shuttled, best I can count, among twenty or so houses with cousins or aunts or grandparents. None of them wanted another kid. It was . . . tough. Sometimes they forgot to feed me. That wasn't as bad as the ones who remembered me too much. The ones who liked to push me around. Told me I was worthless." Jeff rocked on his heels, his eyes on his boots. "By the time I was your age, Noah, I was 'bout the meanest kid you can imagine. Pure anger."

"You? Nah." I almost laughed. "No way. You're like, always mellow."

"*Now.*" Jeff did laugh. "Then, I was more likely to spit in your face than say how-do-you-do. Until Convey. Know what I did first when the old man took me in?" Jeff didn't wait for my answer. "I trashed the Shop, swiped cash from the cashbox, ran away. When my foster caseworker tracked me down—wasn't hard, I was at the closest arcade—he loaded my scrawny butt right back. I wouldn't go in the door. No way this old man was going to tell me what to do. I had been taking care of myself just fine, no matter where they put me."

"What happened?"

"Convey said he wasn't giving up on me. As long as it took me to understand what it meant to be a gentleman, he was going to stay with me. I said, 'Well you better plan on adopting me then, 'cuz it's going to take forever.'" Jeff rubbed the corner of his mouth with his knuckles.

"What happened?" I pushed.

"He adopted me, not that I believed it right away. Truth is, I went out of my way to make the old man miserable. For six straight months, I was grounded, never allowed to leave the old man's sight. He'd walk me into the school, walk me home the end of the day, make me sit on a stool at the Shop, and locked me in my bedroom at night. I hated him. Made sure he knew it, too. But, man, he was good. Made it impossible for me to run.

"We'd toss the ball back and forth in the backyard for hours. *Bam, bam, bam*, just the ball being thrown back and forth. I threw it hard, too, hard as I could. The old man almost always caught it anyway." Jeff tilted his head back against the wall. "And soon? I was talking. It was easier, somehow, to talk while we threw that football back and forth. Each toss, I'd tell about a different house I'd been forced into and out of.

"Enough nights went by and I realized I wasn't talking about where I'd been anymore. I'd talk about where I wanted to go. Told the old man that the second I graduated, I'd be out of there. Off to see the world. Backpack if I had to. Never be tied down to anyone. Just on my own. That was the only time the old man said anything back."

"What'd he say?" I prompted when Jeff didn't pick up the story.

He cleared his throat. "'What about a family?' And I said, 'No way.' But he just laughed and said, 'You just wait.'"

Jeff shifted, slowly rising to his feet. "You know, it's kind of crazy. I don't remember when I started calling him *Dad* or when we stopped needing a football to talk. I hardly remember his voice at all. Just that he listened."

"Did you?" I asked after another long pause.

"Did I what?"

"Did you take off after graduation?"

Jeff shook his head. "Dad was sick by then. Cancer."

Glen had told me once about that, about how Mr. Convey had gotten sick and how Jeff stuck around to take care of him. When he died, Jeff inherited the Shop.

"Do you wish you had left?" I whispered.

Jeff just smiled. "I have everything I need right here." He tilted his head toward the doors. Slowly, I stood.

His hand outstretched to push open the door, Jeff

paused again. "That old man was the first person I've ever trusted. Only one who ever earned my trust. It's— it's tough, even now, to rely on anyone. And he taught me something I carry to my core, Noah. Don't budge. Don't give up on someone you love. And I never will. You're family, Noah. Family doesn't budge."

CHAPTER NINETEEN

A ll around, people sat at round tables. The noise bouncing around the room put the middle school cafeteria to shame. Instead of trays of food and teachers monitoring, people played board games or cards and correctional officers watched over the room for trouble. Seated at each table was a woman in an orange jumpsuit.

My eyes swept the room for Mom. From the way Jeff had acted, I thought I'd hear her before I saw her. He had made it sound as though she'd be tearing down the walls if I weren't in there. But I didn't hear her. And at first, my eyes floated right by where she sat.

Here's the thing: My mom was tiny but tremendous, all at once. She was shorter than me, and so skinny that old ladies at the grocery were always telling her to eat a cupcake. Her hair was a wild, curly mess that always reminded me of a nest, her pale face the egg in the middle. But when you saw her, your mind recognized right away that she was anything but small.

Somehow she could fill up a room. I didn't know

how to explain it. I guess it was like the woodstove in Jeff's living room. Just a black, boxy thing, but warmth poured from it so you felt cozier even if you're on the other side of the room. That was how it was with Mom. Well, when Mom was happy, anyway.

When she was angry, that heat could singe. Just ask Johnny Martins, the fourth grader who swiped the dessert out of my lunchbox every day on the bus back when I was a scrawny second-grade twerp. Mom yelled at the kid the entire way back to his house when she found out. When Johnny ran through his front door, Mom kept on railing against the kid's dad, who was at least the size of a giant and width of a doghouse. The man cowered in front of her. And my Oreos were safe from then on. In fact, Johnny gave me *his* dessert.

But I didn't see that presence anywhere in this would-be cafeteria. Finally I saw Trenton, who spotted me at the same time. He half-stood in the back of the room, waving me toward him. Next to him sat someone who made me think of a tiny bird, perched on the edge of a branch, too terrified to fly. Why was Trenton sitting with this small, pale woman, whose thin arms wrapped around her folded-up knees? But then the woman noticed Trenton's waving and popped to her feet.

"Noah?" I saw her mouth form the words but didn't hear the sound. Her chin wobbled and she held out her arms, but I couldn't move. Jeff poked me, hard, between the shoulder blades, and I stumbled toward her.

Soon—too soon—I stood a few feet from her outstretched hands. "Can I hug her?" I asked Trenton, not remembering the rules.

Then I felt Mom's arms around me. Her chin rested on my shoulder, her hands squeezing across my back. She shook. No, that's not right. It's more like she *vibrated.* Like what I imagine a cloud does before lightning shoots out of it. Mom was like bottled-up energy. Her head tilted against mine. She still smelled like lavender. Maybe it wasn't the shampoo. Maybe it was just her. "Noah," she said again. "I love you."

An officer's heavy steps tapped against the tile as he made his way toward us. Mom glanced over then let her arms trail to my sides. She gripped my hands for a second and then dropped them as the officer moved closer. I wondered why I wasn't feeling anything. "Sit down," she said, and pointed to the chair across from the one she had been sitting on. And suddenly I did feel something: Irritated. Did she really just ask me to have a seat? Like this was one screwed-up tea party?

I guess she saw me gritting my teeth because she snorted. "I know, right?" she said. "I'm acting like a hostess or something. I'm not sure how to act, Noah."

I shrugged and slumped into the seat, looking everywhere but at her.

Trenton coughed. "Ah, Jeff, how 'bout we get some coffee?" He jerked his thumb toward the vending machines lining the back wall of the room.

"Yeah, okay," Jeff said after a small pause. "You want anything, Diane?"

"Um, maybe a Heath bar, if they still have any?" She and Jeff smiled, and I realized there was something there, some hidden joke borne over visits I had refused to go on. "You want anything, Noah?" Mom asked. "They have Starbursts, I think."

I shook my head. "I don't like them anymore," I lied.

"Oh."

Jeff half-reached toward Mom, then let his hand fall. "Be right back," he said. I knew he was glaring at me, but I stared at a scratch in the floor.

"So," Mom said as they left. "I know we have a lot to talk about." I shrugged and rolled my eyes. Mom took a deep breath through her nose. "But I just need to know first—your head? Is it okay? I mean, your last concussion made you a little sleepy, but Jeff said you blacked out this time, and I just need to know—"

"My last concussion?" I broke in. I shouldn't have looked up. Because my eyes caught hers and I couldn't look away.

Mom smiled at me and, for just a second, she grew bigger in my mind. "You wouldn't remember. You were only a toddler. You would hop into a laundry basket,

and I'd push you around the room like it was a race car.
Took a corner too fast and you whapped your head on a
doorframe. God, I panicked. Insisted they admit you to
the hospital for the night, even though the doctor kept
telling me you were okay and it was just a minor thing.
But it was the first time I ever hurt you and—"

This time I didn't need to interrupt her. Everything
that had happened slammed down between us. I went
back to staring at the scratch. Mom's voice dropped to
a whisper. "Certainly wasn't the last time I hurt you,
huh?"

I rolled my eyes.

"You don't want to talk. I get that," she said. "Jeff
tells me you won't even open the letters I've sent. I
can't make up for what I did, Noah. I know that. I can't
imagine how scared you were that night. I feel sick
every time I try. But here's the thing, Noah. I was sick.
I know that now. I had—have—an addiction. I can't
drink alcohol. It makes me a different person, a person
I'm ashamed of." She leaned forward so I'd look at her
again. "In here," she said, "it's not just sitting around
and watching the clock tick, though there's plenty of
that. I've been working with Trenton, going to recovery
meetings. I realize that I can't drink, not ever."

"You've said that before," I muttered. Another
movie started in my mind, full of scenes I had blocked
out before. Images of her sprawled out on the couch,

an empty wine bottle beside her, when I got up in the middle of the night for water, a thick, syrupy smell like a cloud around her. Scenes of her with glassy eyes and dark circles under them in the morning, stumbling around the kitchen to pack me lunch because the alarm didn't wake her. I remembered shivering at a bus stop with her in the winter, waiting for it to take us to day care so she could take another bus to work. She couldn't drive us then because her license had been taken for driving drunk. Each scene ended with the same words: "I'm never drinking again." For a long time, she didn't. That sip of beer with Landon's mom at Sal's was the first time she had since we met Jeff.

"I know you don't believe me, but it's different this time," she said. "I've got a plan. I know where to go for meetings. And you can come, too, if you want. Trenton has this saying, 'All our struggles are family struggles.'"

"Yeah, he's said that to me, too."

Mom bit her lip and nodded at me. After a pause, she said, "Next week, after I'm out, I'm going to take college classes online."

I let my eyes slide to hers.

"I'm going to get a business degree," she said, a smile tugging at her face. "All online, but my counselor says I could get a great job, even with a record like mine."

"That's great," I muttered.

"I'm talking too much about myself." She sighed. "I'm sorry. I want to know what's going on with you. Jeff tells me a lot. He sent me the newspaper. I'm proud of you, honey. That you care that much about the bear."

I had forgotten all about Bucket Bear. Had Ron caught her? I itched to get back to my phone and find out. But I didn't want to leave, either. I know it's stupid, but a part of me felt like the less I said, the longer I could stay there as this bird woman turned back into my mom.

I made my mouth move. "It's nothing. She just needs help, that's all."

"No, it isn't 'nothing.'" Mom's voice hardened. "It's everything to that bear. That's what counts, that you helped."

"Micah came over yesterday," I blurted.

Mom's hands flew to mine. She squeezed my fingers. "Hands off!" the officer barked. "Do that again and visit's over!"

I jerked my hands out of Mom's. She sat on her own hands. "Jeff told me," she said as if the officer hadn't spoken. "Are you okay?"

I chewed my lip, remembering how Micah looked me in the eyes. How he said he forgave me, even though I didn't deserve it. How suddenly it made my chest feel light as air. I nodded. And like a stupid baby, like a weak little boy, my eyes stung and spilled over.

All I wanted, more than anything, was for Mom to put me together again. I wanted to fall toward her. Even though she was smaller than me, I bet my head still fit on her shoulder. I wanted to hear her heart thumping the way I used to when I was little and had a skinned knee or a fever. "Oh, Noah," she whispered.

And I was angry, so, so angry. I didn't want to need her. Not when she put herself in here. Not when she would do something that took her from me.

But her murmured words blanketed me. She was Mom. A frailer, skinnier, less polished Mom. But Mom. And even though I didn't want to, I needed her. Even though she couldn't be there for me. She rocked back and forth slightly, still sitting on her hands, and I knew this was even harder on her. "I'm sorry, Noah. I'm so, so sorry."

I looked her in the eyes, wondering if she could see the boiling anger and sadness inside of me. Instead, a slurry of regret and pain reflected back to me.

"I forgive you," I said, hearing those words echo in Micah's voice.

Mom rocked harder, wrapped her arms around herself instead of me. We stayed like that until Trenton and Jeff came back, arms loaded with candy bars. Jeff dumped a dozen or so candy bars and bags of chips on the table. "Thought we should celebrate," he said. "Looks like things are going well."

Mom and I cracked up.

"Yeah," said Trenton, rocking back on his heels. "So, you ready for next week, Diane?"

Mom wiped her eyes and smoothed her frizzy ponytail. "You mean am I ready to lose the orange jumpsuit?" She smiled at me. "You better believe it. Especially now."

Jeff's gaze shifted to me. I saw the question there. Was *I* ready for Mom to come home? I nodded.

It's funny how a couple hours can be so fast and too slow all at the same time. Too slow because I couldn't think of what to say to her. Every time I looked at her, all I saw was the orange jumpsuit. The officer hovering in the background. The circles under her eyes. Too fast because suddenly our time was up. An officer told us it was time to leave. Mom's goodbye hug was just a quick squeeze. "One more week," she whispered in my ear. "I love you."

Too short because I didn't know what would happen when that week was over. We never got around to talking about what it would be like when she got out. Yeah, I forgave her. But would anyone else? Would she fit back into Jeff's house? My house? My life?

CHAPTER TWENTY

I don't know what made me remember it, but as we drove home from the jail, I kept thinking of this time when I was little—I don't know, maybe five or six—and I ate an entire loaf of bread.

It was the middle of the night. I was hungry, and Mom was asleep on the couch, the television still blaring. She didn't wake up, even when I yelled "I'm hungry!" in her ear. An empty wine bottle was on the floor by the couch. So I found a loaf of white bread in the kitchen—I loved white bread.

Mom wouldn't move so I sat on top of her legs with the bag of bread in my hands. Crusts were gross so I avoided them—I curled my fingers into a fist over the mushy white part and pulled it out. It was so soft I could roll it into a ball, so I did, popping it in my mouth. Again and again and again. Even as my stomach stretched and ached and felt like it was filled with rocks, I grabbed and rolled and ate.

Soon my fingers reached the end of the bag and I had to stop, even though that meant I finally had to feel how thirsty I had become, how full I was. Soon I was crying, great big hiccupping sobs.

Mom finally woke up and saw me, hand in the empty-except-for-crusts bread bag and belly huge. "Noah?" she asked.

I remember holding up the bag. "I ate it all."

Her eyes went to the bottle on the floor. "You and me, my boy. We've got to work on our limits." And then I threw up all over her legs.

What's sticking in my mind, though, is the bread left in the bag. Just the crusts, piled on top of each other with the centers gone.

That's how I felt as we left the jail. Like someone had reached in and scooped out everything soft inside me, leaving just the crust.

Ron had texted me while I was visiting Mom. *No go on Bucket Bear. Slipped away. Time to turn in the towel, kid.*

I texted him back. *Don't give up yet. Please.*

His reply beeped in a second later. *Bear was downright bony.*

Again I typed: *Don't give up on her.*

Ron didn't reply until we were halfway home.

It's been months. We've got limited resources. The bear's not going to make it. Enough is enough.

★

Landon was on the porch when we got home. I had forgotten about him wanting to track the bear with me. "Don't stay out late," Jeff said as I opened the car door. It was the first time he spoke since we got in the car.

"I won't."

"And, Noah?" Jeff grabbed my coat sleeve, keeping me in place.

"Yeah?"

"I need to tell you something." Jeff raked his hand down his face. "You asked if I was keeping you out of guilt. I'm not. But I do feel guilty. More guilty than you can imagine."

I closed the door, holding up a finger to Landon to wait. He nodded and went back to playing a game on his phone. "Well, knock it off."

"No, let me finish." Jeff turned off the engine and turned toward me. "I went there, to the party. I tried to get her to give me her keys. When she didn't, I just left. I left *you* there, Noah. That's why I feel guilty."

"It's all right," I said.

"It isn't. But I'll keep making up for it."

"You don't have to," I said. "I mean, I think you have by now."

"That's the thing, kid," Jeff said and smiled. "I *want* to. I like having you around."

"I like having you around," I said, even though it felt awkward.

"Cool."

"Cool."

"I know I'm not your dad." Jeff picked at a grease stain on his nail. "But . . . I wish I were."

"Me, too," I whispered.

"All right, get out of here before we start hugging and sharing our feelings."

Being around Landon was even more awkward than the conversation with Jeff. It started out with Landon showing me all these images of bear prints on his phone. I took him around back and pointed out the tracks in the mud.

I knew it was useless—Ron had tromped all through there just a couple hours before and came up empty—and I think Landon knew it, too. But we kept going.

"So you and Rina?" Landon asked. "Are you, like, a thing?"

I shrugged. "She's cool, when you get to know her."

Landon raised an eyebrow, but didn't say anything.

The tracks ended near the stream. So many footprints merged there, we couldn't make out the bear's anymore. The light rain was just enough to turn everything to a muddy mess. I checked the websites for any Bucket Bear sightings. Nothing since this morning.

"Maybe no one could find it today because some-how it got the bucket off? Like maybe it's just fine now," Landon said.

"Maybe," I said, even though I knew it wasn't true. *Enough is enough.*

"So," Landon said as we gave up and headed home, the hoods on our sweatshirts up and tight around our faces. "How was it?"

I knew he meant visiting Mom. I let my head fall back so rain pattered against my face, hoping it would help words to describe the day take root and grow in my mind. After a while, I just shook my head. "She comes home in a week."

"At least she comes home, man." And I knew he was thinking of his dad.

Back at the gate, Landon shoved his hands in his pockets. We stood there for a minute, awkward again. Should I invite him in? Or was this a one-time mercy thing to make up for the concussion? Jeff came to the back porch.

"See you at school?" Landon asked.

"Yeah," I nodded. "See you."

CHAPTER TWENTY-ONE

The longest week of school in the history of time crawled to a close Friday with an assembly. Again, Mr. Anderson called us out to the (former) football field. It was frosty enough for his breath to make clouds that drifted over us as he spoke on the makeshift stage.

Rina shivered next to me, and pulled knit mittens out of her enormous backpack. "What?" she said when I raised an eyebrow.

"That bag, it's like the one on the kids' show. You know, where the nanny keeps pulling furniture out of it?"

Rina yanked on the end of a scarf, toppling notebooks, pens, and books out of the bag in the process. The scarf was long enough to reach her ankles. "Just for that, I'm not sharing."

I crossed my arms. Without wanting to, my eyes scanned the woods. I knew there wasn't much hope for the bear. Ron had stopped answering my texts and emails, sending every message to voicemail.

"No sightings posted on any of our sites," Rina said quietly. Figures she'd know I was looking for the bear.

I nodded, now looking straight ahead again. "Yeah. I know."

"Sorry, Noah," she added.

"Whatever. It's just a bear."

Rina moved a half step closer to me, so our arms pressed against each other. "Hey, when are you getting your mom tomorrow?"

My stomach seized up at her words. Mom was coming home tomorrow. It didn't feel real. I couldn't imagine her just being home, hanging out around the kitchen table, going to the grocery store. It didn't feel real. "Not until late afternoon."

"Cool. I'll come over in the morning."

"What? Why?"

Rina heaved a trademark sigh. "For the newspaper. We have to get started on the next edition."

I opened my mouth, but Rina covered it with her mitten. "Don't even say it," she warned. "You're in this newspaper club for the long haul, bear or no bear. If you want to stick with the animal beat, that's cool. Ron called yesterday and said we're experiencing an influx of raccoons in the area."

"What?" I said into Rina's mitten.

"Yeah." Rina lowered her hand, but locked me in

place with narrowed eyes. "He says raccoons are flocking to the area. Seems people are leaving out food, mostly around places where Bucket Bear had been spotted. He even asked if I knew anything about it."

I shifted a little and pointed toward the stage. "Looks like Mr. Anderson's about to start."

Rina stepped so she was square in front of me again. "Ron wanted to know if we were leaving food out for the bear. I told him not to be ridiculous, that feeding a wild animal is dangerous and stupid." She jabbed a mittened thumb into my chest. "Really stupid."

"I'll stop, all right?" I snapped. "She's dead, anyway."

Rina sighed again, this one just a sad puff of air. "Probably. But it's weird they haven't found a body. I guess, anyway. I mean, you don't really hear about bear bodies being found and you'd think they die all the time. I wonder if she found a cave or something."

I swallowed but didn't say anything.

"Sorry." Rina's face flushed. "I am, really. It's just that keeps getting to me. I get that the bear was savvy about getting away from all of us. But if she died, you'd think we would've found her. Ron said disposing of that big bear that was hit by the tractor trailer two months ago was a huge pain."

"Rina, stop." I rubbed at my eyes with the heels of my hands, trying to smudge out the image of the bear wasting away alone. I bent over a little as my stomach churned.

"You have a surprisingly delicate stomach," Rina pointed out.

"Nothing about me is delicate."

Rina snorted.

Anything else Rina would've said was cut off by Mr. Anderson. "You're probably wondering why I've called you all out here on this frosty morning," he yelled into the microphone. "Well, I have an important announcement, and it just had to be shared here."

Grinning, Mr. Anderson beckoned and Brenna, in her little cheerleading uniform, bounded onto the stage. Even though it was so cold her knees shook, Brenna clapped as she bounced to the front. "Give me a 'B'!" she shouted.

The cluster of kids around me roared. "*B!*" Brenna continued spelling out the Bruins. Even Rina chirped in a little, knocking me with her elbow when I waggled another eyebrow at her.

"Whatever," she muttered but her smile stretched.

I snickered and bent to root through her bag.

"What are you doing?" she yelped.

"Looking for an orange-and-black Bruins sweatshirt. I'm sure you've got one in here!"

"I do not!" Rina yelled and pushed my hands off the backpack with a laugh. Suddenly she froze, her eyes locking in on something in the distance.

"What?" I turned to look where her eyes had snagged.

Nothing but trees.

"Nothing." Rina shook her head. "Just a shadow, I guess." She grabbed a notebook and pen out of her bag and started scribbling notes for the assembly. "Better pay attention," she said as I scanned the tree line for what had gotten her attention. "You could be assigned this story."

Mr. Anderson took the microphone back from Brenna, who kept right on clapping as she trotted off the stage. "Our fund-raiser was successful! We raised five hundred dollars for MADD! And I got word this week that at tomorrow's TriCounty Football League meeting, the Ashtown Bruins will officially be allowed back in the game next season. Congratulations for your hard work and for raising awareness for MADD!"

All around us, people went nuts. The loudest, of course, was Landon.

"Starting next fall," Mr. Anderson continued, "we will reestablish our football team. So pack up those buckets, kids. Please. And go, Bruins!"

My stomach twisted again. Stupid me. Here I thought with Micah forgiving me, with me forgiving Mom, that I'd stop feeling sick every time I thought of the Bruins. I thought I had dealt with it. Stupid me.

Because as soon as the crowd roared again, my ears rang with the sound of a crash. All I saw were blurs. All I felt was a rush and a fall.

And right then and there—right when everything was getting better for everyone—I threw up.

"Like I said, delicate stomach," Rina murmured.

Mr. Davies walked me into the building to get to the nurse's office. He stood about two feet away from me and kept shaking his head.

"What?" I snapped. I mean, seriously, it's bad enough to be doing the walk of shame with puke crusted on your shirt. Having a teacher you hate smirking and rolling his eyes at everyone you pass is beyond the realm of tolerable situations. (Yeah, I know. I sound like Rina.)

Mr. Davies snorted. "You just can't stand not being the center of attention, can you, Mr. Brickle?"

"What are you talking about?"

"It goes back to that whole survival of fittest thing. Here was a chance for you to adapt—to cheer along the new team—and instead you upchuck all over the place. Suddenly no one's cheering the Bruins anymore. They're back to being disgusted by you."

My mouth soured again. I knew he was right. This wasn't just a quiet little upset stomach. I pretty much sprayed everyone around me. Distractedly, I hoped Rina had a change of clothes in that massive backpack of hers. Landon wasn't in the range of fire, but he was close enough to see. Was he back to hating me again?

I stumbled a step, and Mr. Davies shook his head again. "Speaking of survival, whatever happened to your bear?"

I didn't say anything, just concentrated on the silver lining Mr. Davies had shared earlier that week—that he was heading to a conference over the weekend and wouldn't be back until the middle of next week.

"Like I said," he went on, as though I had spoken, "some animals are just too stupid to live."

Saturday morning, the whirl of the vacuum cleaner woke me before the sun. I might've gotten a half hour of sleep. Partly it was because I knew it was the last night I'd be in the house without Mom. Mostly it was because of Jeff.

After he picked me up Friday afternoon, Jeff went nuts scrubbing the kitchen cabinets with a washrag and soap. "Don't throw up on anything," he warned, even though my stomach hadn't bothered me again. The bathroom was spotless, even all the old magazines thrown away and extra toilet paper stacked above the tank. The whole house smelled like Lysol. I went to the pantry for a snack and thought Jeff was going to bite my head off. "Don't you eat standing like that! I just scrubbed the floor!"

I moved to the table.

"I just washed that, too!" he said. We both stared at the only thing messy still on the table—the enormous pile of unopened letters. I grabbed a garbage bag from under the sink and shook it out. Just as I was about to sweep them all into it, Jeff said, "Noah, are you sure . . . "

I nodded, dumping all the letters, then twisting the bag. "I'm going to put these in my closet. Maybe Mom will want to read them someday."

Jeff ran his knuckles along his jaw. "Or you. Someday you might be ready."

I shrugged.

I ended up eating some tortilla chips on the back porch. I heard some shuffling and squeaking under the porch and tried not to think about what Rina had said about the raccoons.

Jeff was washing the windows when I came inside. His cleaning streak went right on into the night.

We ate at Sal's, and Jeff ordered an extra dozen hot wings to bring home. "You know Diane loves hot wings," he said with a grin.

"But only if they're cold," I finished for him. "And only for breakfast."

Jeff smiled. I tried to ignore the way his eyes were too bright, too watery. It felt nice to talk about her in the present, instead of just how things used to be. I swallowed around the lump lodged in my throat. *She's coming home.* I was starting to believe it, I guess.

As soon as we got home, Jeff went back to work, this time dusting off the blades of the kitchen ceiling fan. Then he noticed how that just sent dust down on the already-scrubbed table and he cleaned that again.

"She's just going to be happy to be home," I pointed out. "I mean, I don't think she's going to going around looking for dust bunnies, Dad."

Jeff froze, big D-A-D spelled out invisibly in the air above him, wet washrag dripping down his arm. After a couple seconds of him being a statue and my face flaming, he softly added, "I just want it to be nice for her. For all of us." When he turned to face me, his eyes were bright all over again.

And now, the vacuum cleaner was out all over again.

I stumbled out to the kitchen to grab a Pop-Tart that I'd have to eat on the porch.

"We need to leave in fifteen!" Jeff called over the din of the vacuum cleaner.

"But Mom isn't getting out until three!"

"Yeah, but we gotta stop by the Shop first. I scheduled a couple quick oil changes in the morning, then we're closing 'til Monday."

I fired a text to Rina, telling her to meet me at the Shop instead of at home.

"Have to check in with the girlfriend?" Jeff asked.

"Shut up."

To tell the truth, I wasn't all that sure Rina would show up. I mean, I *did* throw up on her and all. But she already was perched on the bench outside the Shop when we pulled up in Jeff's truck. Even though it was November, sun warmed the air enough to not need more than a sweatshirt.

"Want to talk out here?" I asked as Jeff went into the Shop.

"Sure." She jerked her chin toward the woods beside the Shop. "Just aim that way if you're going to get sick again."

"Sorry about that." I sat down next to her on the bench and was glad she didn't scoot away.

"No prob." Rina kicked at the backpack by her feet. "I had a change of clothes in my bag."

We had just plotted out the next issue—actually, Rina had plotted; I nodded and took notes—when Jeff came out of the Shop, flipping the OPEN sign to CLOSED. "All right, got everything squared away. Ready to go get your mom, Noah?"

Rina shifted so her arm was against mine.

My stomach clenched, just for a second, but Jeff saw my grimace. "Noah?"

"Already?" I asked. Bitterness filled my mouth again.

I'm so freaking stupid. I *wanted* her to come home. I did. I wanted her to check my homework, to kiss the top of my head as she walked by, to hear her laugh, to see her smile. I wanted her to sleep in the next room and be the first person I saw when I woke up. I wanted it so bad my knees turned to water when I thought about it.

But I *didn't* want everything to change. Or even to go back to what it was. I didn't want Jeff to stop being my parent. I didn't want to watch to see whether she was drinking again. I didn't want to see people's faces shift when they saw her next. I didn't want to have to run my plans for after school by her.

I forgave her. I did. But that didn't mean it was okay. That I was okay. Everything was so stupid, so messy, so mixed up. And it was all over. I was all out of time.

"Noah—"

Just then, a car with a hiccupping motor and billowing gray smoke pulled into the Shop.

CHAPTER TWENTY-TWO

The car shuddered to a stop right behind Jeff's truck. "Sorry!" called Jeff, waving his arms to get the driver's attention. "We're closed!" He swore under his breath when the engine shut off.

The car door opened but I couldn't make out the driver behind the cloud of smoke. But as soon as he spoke, I knew just who it was. "No, no! You've got to fix this thing! I've got to be at a conference in Alexandria in a couple hours!"

"Mr. Davies?" Rina asked.

For a second, Mr. Davies stalled. The desperate look on his face wiped away and his usual cocky smirk appeared. His eyes flicked between Rina, me, and Jeff. Finally, Mr. Davies's gaze settled on Jeff. "I need you to fix this right away. I have someplace to be."

Jeff's jaw clenched. "Sorry, man. But so do we."

"Listen, *man*," Mr. Davies spat. "I'm attending an important conference. I cannot be late. This is the only auto shop in town and this car isn't making it anywhere." He pulled out a worn leather wallet. "What's it going to take?"

"I'd say a tow truck," Jeff quipped. "You're blocking me in."

"Then you've got to fix it!" The cocky smirk disappeared for a second. "Please, just help me out." Mr. Davies shuffled so his back was to me and Rina. His voice dipped, so Rina and I leaned forward to catch his words. "My boss is already threatening to can me. My job's on the line here."

Jeff grit his teeth. His chin jerked up a millimeter. "I'll take a look," he said, "but if I can't get this thing running in a half hour, I'm putting her in neutral and pushing it out of the way."

Stepping past Mr. Davies toward me, Jeff squeezed my shoulder. "A half hour, Noah. Then we're leaving."

I sank back onto the bench.

"How are you feeling?" Rina asked. "I know there's a lot going on for you . . . your mom, and the stuff with the bear, too."

I huffed out my nose and stared off toward the trees, trying to pull my tie-dyed feelings into straight lines again. "I feel like . . . I'm too much like her."

"Oh, the bear," Rina said. "Like you can't shake consequences of a past decision? Sort of like how the bear has something choking her? And that you can't really take in what's going on because you're partially blinded by what's already happened to you, the way the bucket keeps the bear from seeing?"

I stared at her. "I meant my mom."

"Oh."

"That I make stupid, selfish decisions, like my mom."

"Oh. Sorry."

I stared into the woods again, thinking about what Rina said. I heard twigs snapping. Then a shadow took shape just inside the woods. And I took off running. "The bear!"

"Noah! Wait!"

But I didn't. I couldn't. She was just in front of me!

Rina didn't follow me. She ran into the Shop. I dimly heard her yelling for Jeff and Mr. Davies. Soon I heard Jeff bellowing. "Noah! Get back here!"

I did stop. But only because the bear was right in front of me.

She faced me, dragging in air through her snout. Maybe it was the bucket that amplified the sound, turning the growl that came next into a roar that seemed to rumble through me. I could just spy her mouth hanging open to reveal a tongue splattered with blue. Huffing, snorting, she shook her head back and forth as she tried to take me in.

"It's okay," I whispered. "It's okay."

I stepped slowly toward her. She pawed at the

ground and stepped back, but didn't run like I thought she would, even as Jeff, Mr. Davies, and Rina crashed through the woods behind us.

She rose up her back feet, slamming down her front paws and making a creaking, grunting snort. Head swinging again, she turned toward the woods. She was on the verge of running. I knew it. But she was so weak. It was like a war going on in inside of her, I think. Mr. Davies's lecture on animals' instincts for fight or flight whispered in my head. As the three of them got closer to us, I could see flight winning out.

This was it. We were both out of time.

So I did something really stupid.

I jumped on the bear.

The bear stood for a minute, shaking all over. Her head reared back, and I knew she would've ripped into me if her head wasn't muzzled by the bucket. "Noah!" Jeff stormed. He threw himself at us and grabbed my arms, trying to rip me off of her.

"You've got to help her!" I screamed into his face. "Help her!" The bear shuddered under me, and fell to her side. She kept grunting, but it was wheezy and desperate. She clawed at the air. "Do something!"

Jeff's eyes locked with mine over the bear. He grabbed at the bucket and yanked. The bear cried out in another creaking groan, but the bucket didn't budge. Jeff gripped the bear, his hands over mine. "You let go," he ordered me. "I need you to run into the Shop and grab some bolt cutters." Jeff looked up at Mr. Davies. "You! Help me hold down the bear."

"You can't be serious."

"Do it!" I had never heard Jeff yell before. For just a second, I saw the furious kid Trenton had described.

I guess Mr. Davies did, too, because he flipped his tie over his shoulder and leaned over the bear, holding her down with Jeff. I paused half a second then tore off to the Shop. I was back in under a minute, bolt cutters in hand. Rina stood to the side on her phone, trying to reach Ron.

"Now, listen," said Jeff, his voice steady again. "You're going to have to get close to her, but I want you behind her head. I'm holding her head down. You're going to wedge the cutters under the edge of this plastic. Cut and pull. And do it quick."

"So she can't get away?" I asked, already leaning in. I had to put my knee above her leg to get the cutters under the plastic.

"That, and we're going to be late," Jeff muttered.

"My conference!" Mr. Davies moaned.

"Shut up!" Jeff and I said at the same time.

I threw my body into the cutter and it only made a small dent in the plastic. I did it again and again. The dent turned into a wedge. With one arm, Jeff yanked on the side of the bucket, pulling it farther apart. The muscles in his neck strained and his arm looked like corded rope. Quickly, I lined up the cutters and yanked the blades together as Jeff pulled.

"It's working!" Rina cheered. I glanced at her. She held the phone toward us, filming.

Beneath us, the bear quivered, like she could tell she was almost free. Again, Jeff yanked and I cut.

At the exact same time, the bear twisted her head back, bucking against our grips and pulling her head free. All three of us fell back as the bear—who had seemed so small a second earlier—got to her feet and suddenly loomed over us. She didn't stop though, didn't pause a second, just ripped off into the woods as we cheered.

Rina jumped up and down, still filming, as Jeff grabbed me with both muddy, scratched-up arms and crushed me against him. "Don't you ever do that again," he whispered. "I could've lost you. Do you understand?"

I hugged him back.

"You did it! You saved her! I can't wait to post this video!" Rina yelled.

Mr. Davies stood and wiped at the mud caking his pants and sleeves. "Good, because I'm going to need an excuse for Mr. Anderson for why I didn't show at the conference."

We all turned toward Mr. Davies, and for a second

none of us spoke, just stared at him. There was a dark wet spot, stretching out from the groin area of Mr. Davies's pants. Rina tilted her head and then arched an eyebrow at me.

At the same time, Mr. Davies realized what we were looking at and crossed his hands over his pants. "I got scared, okay? Don't tell me you didn't nearly pee your pants!"

Rina swung the camera toward Jeff and me. I grinned. "Can't say I did, Mr. Davies."

"You know what? That's it. I quit. I quit!" Mr. Davies threw his hands in the air and marched back to his car.

Somehow, we made it to the jail in time.

Rina, her face glowing and smile huge, had thrown her arms around me in a tight squeeze even though I was covered in mud. She promised to also post the video on all of Bucket Bear's sites.

Jeff and I rushed home, changed clothes, cleaned up, and got on the road. Yeah, there was still mud caked in the back of my head. I was sure Jeff's scratches stung under the sweater he threw on. But we made it.

On the way, Jeff told me that it wasn't actually a bucket that had trapped the bear. "That was a maxi. It's a kind of air bag on tractor trailers that cushions between the cab and trailer. Somehow she got one wedged on her head."

It wasn't a bucket. It hadn't been my fault all along. None of it had been my fault.

But that didn't matter. It didn't take away from how good it felt to have helped her.

That's what counts, Mom's words echoed in my head, *that you helped.*

I told Jeff about the huge bear that had been taken out by a truck a couple months earlier. "I bet that was her mother. I kept wondering why such a small bear didn't have a mother hanging around."

Jeff nodded. "That would explain why the bear got tangled up in the maxi. Mom got in trouble and her kid paid for it." He sighed softly. "Guess you can relate. Both of you too stubborn to let anyone help you until it was almost too late."

"You're the second person to compare me to that bear."

"Rina's a smart girl."

We were quiet for a long time. "Do you think she's going to be okay?" I asked as Jeff put the truck in park outside the jail. He didn't ask—and I didn't know— whether we were still talking about the bear.

He nodded. "The whole experience weakened her. But she's tough. She's a fighter. She's going to be okay."

For a second, we sat in silence, staring at the building. "You ready?" he asked.

"I'm ready."

ACKNOWLEDGMENTS

A couple years ago, I saw a story on the news about a small black bear in Clarion County, Pennsylvania, with what appeared to be a bucket wedged on its head. The townspeople spotted this bear over the course of several weeks, alerting animal services, setting up a "Save The Bucket Bear" Facebook page, and even attempting to help the bear themselves. In the end, several of them tackled this bear, holding it down while others used tools to set it free.

A few weeks later, I told my agent I wanted to write a redemption story about a boy trapped by his mistakes and fear. Thank you, Nicole Resciniti, super agent and beautiful friend, for believing in me even when I quietly added that it'd also be about a bear with a bucket stuck on its head. Nic, you're just the best.

I'm also grateful for Jeff Rowe, a family friend and lawyer, who connected me with public defender Greta Davis of north central Pennsylvania. Greta was so generous with her time, explaining to me what Noah's mom would face in the legal system. Any mistakes in that portrayal, here, are mine alone. When I had questions about sponsorship, Greta connected me with Louis Ortenzio of Celebrate Recovery in Northern West Virginia. Lou's open heart and powerful message is inspiring change among so many families in the area, giving them the strength they need to manage addiction, incarceration and stigma. Though he's no longer a doctor, he remains a healer, and it was a privilege to talk with him.

Thank you also to Deputy Warden Sandie Barone, who offered insight into what Noah's visits with his incarcerated mom would be like. Again, any mistakes in that process are on me.

Many, many thanks to the best critique partners a writer could dream of having—Susan Jennings Haller, Lynn Rush, Buffy Andrews, and Emma Vrabel. I love you, ladies. Thank you to Ben Vrabel for the expert insight into soccer stars and football plays.

I'm especially grateful for Sky Pony Press for launching my career and continuing to support powerful stories. Thank you doesn't seem enough for editor Becky Herrick, for believing in Noah's story and making it stronger. I appreciate everyone on the incredible Sky Pony team, including editorial director Alison Weiss, production editor Joshua Barnaby, copy editor Bethany Bryan, cover designer Kate Gartner, and Emma Dubin. Thank you also to Adrienne Szpyrka for being first to fight for Noah.

ABOUT THE AUTHOR

Beth Vrabel is the award-winning author of *A Blind Guide to Stinkville*, *A Blind Guide to Normal*, *Caleb and Kit*, and the Pack of Dorks series. She can't clap to the beat or be trusted around Nutella, but indulges in both often, much to the dismay of her family. She lives in the Dallas, Texas area. Visit her online at www.bethvrabel.com.